The Nought

Jeffrey Thomas

The Nought

DARK MOONS

ISBN: 978-1-888993-81-3

Interior and cover design by César Puch
Editor and Publisher, Joe Morey

DARK MOONS

Dark Moons
an imprint of Weird House Press
Central Point, OR 97502
www.weirdhousepress.com

Part One

The Colony

It was happening again. *God help us*, Zhen might have thought … if she believed in deities. But she believed only in nothingness—as did the Nought.

Colonist Vardon Grigoryan had come into the medical unit complaining that his head was killing him, his face shiny with sweat, his body visibly shaking.

"My arms hurt, too," he said, holding them out in front of him, but with his long sleeves all Zhen saw was their shaking. "Like I've pulled every muscle in them!"

"Come in here, Mr. Grigoryan," Zhen instructed, gesturing toward the adjacent imaging room. She intended to give him a thorough med scan, but she already feared the worst.

As Vardon stepped ahead of her, Zhen threw a look back at her supervisor, Florence. Like Zhen, Florence had an attractive face with Asian features, but she only looked back at Zhen blankly.

As soon as Vardon had stretched out on the narrow scan table, however, the spasms began … in an eye blink escalating into full-blown convulsions. Vardon thrashed wildly, flinging his head from side to side and screaming, "No! Oh no! Please don't let it happen to me! Hurry, put me into cryo! Put me in cryo before—"

But it was much too late for that, if such a move would even have halted the transformation.

Zhen punched the key to slide shut the transparent cylinder that would enclose Vardon on the scan table. Remembering how violent the previous victims had become, she hoped to contain the man before he could hurt someone … but the clear cover was gliding into place too slowly. Vardon bunched up his legs, rolled out from under the closing cover, and dropped to the floor. The scan cylinder sealed shut with no one inside it.

"Mr. Grigoryan!" Zhen cried, taking an instinctive step toward him.

He was on hands and knees, his back hunched and flinching hard, his backbone pressing against the fabric of his shirt as if the vertebrae themselves were being pushed up. As Zhen reached out a hand to him, Vardon raised his head and looked back at her over his shoulder. When she saw his vein-covered face—with its bulging eyes and distended, drooling tongue—she withdrew her hand sharply and gasped.

Vardon screamed again, but this time it was a horrifyingly inhuman sound, and in that instant his face erupted. The spray of blood spattered Zhen's green medical scrubs.

That was when she turned to flee from the imaging room. "Florence!" she yelled. "Call security!" She hoped to get through the door and close it securely before Vardon could rise to his feet, turn, and come at her … but she remembered that the imaging room door had no lock.

Then, Vardon was on her.

In the other room, which acted as the reception area and front office for the colony's medical unit, Florence had immediately heeded Zhen's cry and got security on the front desk's main com screen, reporting: "There's a, uh, a violent patient in the med unit. They're, ah … changing. I repeat, a violent patient in the med unit … please hurry … they're, um, changing."

Then, just as Florence was rising from the desk to go provide assistance in restraining the out-of-control patient, Florence heard Zhen give out a bloodcurdling—if short-lived—scream.

Florence covered the distance to the imaging room as quickly as possible, but upon reaching its door paused a moment in the threshold to absorb the scene inside.

The colonist named Vardon Grigoryan was hunched low over Zhen, who lay on her back on the floor, silent and unmoving with her limbs splayed. Vardon's back with its strangely distended spine blocked Florence's view of Zhen's head, but around this obstacle Florence could see a glassy pool of blood, spreading in size.

"Oh dear," Florence said. And then: "Mr. Grigoryan, what have you done?"

Upon detecting Florence behind him—perhaps his ears still worked, despite his new deformities?—Vardon rose to his full height, spun around, and rushed straight at Florence.

"No," Florence protested, "you must remain here! I can't let you—"

But Vardon slammed the ends of both his arms straight into Florence's chest, and Florence staggered backwards, while still managing to remain standing. Vardon then pushed past Florence, obviously headed for the med unit's door … beyond which lay the rest of the colony.

"No, Mr. Grigoryan," Florence persisted, reaching out quickly enough to snatch hold of the back of the man's shirt. "Let me help you! Perhaps a, uh, sedative will—"

As if enraged at Florence's attempt to stop him, Vardon again whipped around, and this time gave Florence a powerful backhanded blow. Again Florence stumbled back, but this time overbalanced and fell to the floor.

Spinning away from Florence, Vardon Grigoryan once more turned his attention to the med unit's door. He went to it, and it sensor caused it to open automatically at his presence. But at the same time the door slid back, a security team member outfitted in a black uniform and black full-head helmet was revealed outside in the corridor. He had arrived at that very second, having been stationed nearby for just such an emergency as this.

Vardon let out a wet-sounding roar at having his path blocked, but this expression of outrage was cut short as the security guard thrust out his drawn handgun—a powerful Wolff .45—and discharged it once, pointblank, into Vardon's chest. The entrance wound was bad enough but the exit wound was worse.

Still lying on the floor, somewhat stunned, Florence looked up to see Vardon blown backwards, to hit the floor himself a short distance away. It was Florence's impression that the soldier had shot Vardon more out of fear, at the abrupt sight of his transfigured state, than out of a sense of threat.

Vardon Grigoryan was number four.

Part Two

Antarctica

- 1 -

The more time Captain Robert Fuseli spent on Earth, the more convinced he became that he was no fan of the planet. Of course, it wasn't the planet itself but its people, and so the fewer of those grouped in one area the better—and nowhere on Earth were fewer people grouped than at its South Pole.

However, the woman currently sitting astride an idling hoversled beside Fuseli's identical sled had a markedly less enthusiastic view of Antarctica. Rhan Luyen flipped open her helmet's tinted face shield, squinting against the bite of icy air and the glare of the sun reflecting off the awe-inspiring expanse of snow. In this way, she revealed the face with its strong cheekbones and intense dark eyes that Fuseli had immediately been struck by upon meeting her. Though, he'd seen those eyes look happier.

"Fun, huh?" Fuseli said to her with exaggerated cheer, having slid open his own face shield. Together, they'd been riding their twin hoversleds across a flat landscape of snow-encrusted ice several miles deep, which only seemed to end where it met the harsh blue of sky. Here at the bottom of the world, there was only one six-month-long day and one six-month-long night, and right now it was day's turn to reign.

"Sure, I love it here," Rhan said. "It's just like back home. And by home, I mean Titania."

Rhan was a stranger not just to Antarctica, but to this dimension.

Last year there had been a catastrophic accident involving research into interplanetary teleportation, in which a number of extradimensional entities had accidently been torn from their respective worlds and deposited at the research station on Titania, the largest moon of Uranus. A military medical officer with the Colonial Forces, Fuseli had been summoned to investigate the situation, and it had been concluded that Rhan's actual home was an alternate version of Earth, in a less technologically advanced state. So far, no efforts to establish the location of that alternate Earth in space-time had proved successful, and Rhan held little hope of ever being restored to her own world.

"At least it isn't as dark here," Fuseli pointed out, smiling.

"And it won't be for a long time. After which, it'll be even more like Titania."

"You wouldn't be able to lift that face shield on Titania," Fuseli said.

"There is that, I guess. But I'm so cold already I think I'd better put it back down, before my nose turns black and rots off." She did lower the shield back in place, so Fuseli followed suit, but they continued their conversation over their helmet mics.

"I hate when that happens," Fuseli agreed.

"This little joyride is supposed to feel like freedom to me?" Rhan asked.

"You could escape," Fuseli said, gesturing toward that hard line where whiteness and blueness met. "Just keep going thataway."

"Sure, sure, Robert," Rhan said. "But if I did, would you shoot me?" She nodded at Fuseli's midsection. She knew he wore a handgun in a belt holster under his heated outer jacket.

"Come on, the gun's not for you. You never know when a terrorist group or enemy government is going to attack, even at a remote spot like this."

"And them?" Rhan hooked her thumb over her shoulder. Keeping a discreet distance behind them, but not so distant that they couldn't rush to the pair's aid if needed, were two Colonial Forces security people resting astride their own idling hoversleds. "Would *they* shoot me, if you didn't?"

"Rhan ... you're in a mood. Look, if you bolted and tried to escape I'd just tackle you. Though, God knows what that might lead to."

"It would lead to something of yours turning black and rotting off."

"I hate when *that* happens."

"Seriously, Robert … how much longer here? I've lost track of time. Especially with this nonstop daylight."

"I'm sorry, Rhan, but I told you at the start … this was inevitable."

"But why *here?* There has to be research bases in cities where it's actually warm. Or even in the country."

"Rhan, there isn't much country left to speak of on Earth … at least, not anywhere that's safe. This world isn't like the one you came from. I think I need to show you more vids to get it across. Wars, pollution, crime, disease, starvation. Technology can't keep up with the battle. The people out there are full of fear and hate … dangerous hunger and despair. That's why we've taken to the stars." He snorted bitterly. "So we can spread that cancer outward, instead of curing an incurable host."

"So you think we were better off on Titania."

"I'm not saying there aren't less inhospitable research bases, and you'll get to see some of them. Other teams still want their turn with the amazing extradimensional lady. But for now, this is it—and I had no say in the location. I'm just glad they've let me stay with you up to now, to help with all their endless interviews and examinations."

"I know you like examining me," she quipped.

"Endlessly, but purely in the interest of science. Anyway … it's not an accident they chose this particular base. They felt you'd be secure here."

"In case I decided I did want to test my freedom."

"Rhan. They're protecting you."

"Protecting me like a lab rat, you mean. In a glass cage with an impressive view. Or is that a *depressive* view?"

"I guess we should go back, huh?" he sighed.

"What? No picnic lunch out here?"

"I know this isn't easy for you, Rhan."

"And I know you're doing your best to keep me happy, Robert," she said. He saw her finally smile behind the face shield. "In *every* way." Then she jerked around in the saddle to look toward their security tail. "They're not listening in on our conversation, are they?"

"No," Fuseli chuckled. "Not unless I open their channel."

"Captain Fuseli," said a voice inside Fuseli's helmet at that very moment, the timing almost causing him to flinch. "You're being called back to the station, sir. A ship is coming in and you're requested."

Fuseli twisted around atop his vehicle, which floated a little above the snow, to look back in the direction of Research Base Amundsen-Scott. This base had changed a lot over many years, its sprawling main structure looming above the frozen desolation on thick legs that could be adjusted to keep it level, and sufficiently above the changeable snow. Approaching a series of elevated landing pads and hangars, set off a bit from the main structure, came a common military helicraft called a Harbinger. A number of these well-armed craft were always posted at the base anyway, to protect it from potential attack. Fuseli hadn't exaggerated the state of the world to Rhan.

"Who is it?" Fuseli said into his mic. He saw Rhan watching him, though this conversation was on a security channel she wasn't privy to.

"Can't say on this channel, sir, sorry."

So it was a bigshot. "I'm coming in." Fuseli cut the call, turned to wave to the two security people who'd been tailing him and Rhan, and pointed them toward the science research station. Then he reopened his channel with Rhan. "Joyride's over," he told her.

- 2 -

Inside Research Base Amundsen-Scott, Rhan had glanced back at Fuseli over her shoulder as she headed off for the cafeteria to eat lunch without him. He knew she'd sit at a table alone, projecting a force field of resentment to keep others at bay. She hadn't warmed up sufficiently to any of the base's research staff, having told Fuseli she always suspected them of *observing* her even when she was taking meals or spending time with or without him in the gym or rec room. Though more sad than reproachful, that backwards glance made Fuseli feel even guiltier than he already did, as he turned in another direction once inside the base, toward a long corridor that would take him to what was essentially the base's miniature airport. The two security guards that had accompanied Fuseli and Rhan stayed with him, and he wondered if that was now more to protect the unnamed newcomer from *him* rather than him from the newcomer.

Once he reached the airport area, he saw that the newcomer already had a security detail of his own: four men and/or women (it was hard to tell, bulky with black chest armor as they were, and black-visored full-head helmets) carrying bulky Drang assault engines, also black.

Once inside the base, Fuseli had stripped out of his own helmet and heated outerwear. He presently wore a camouflaged uniform in white and gray arctic patterns, and the black beret that identified him as a member of Special Ops. Fuseli was fifty-one, with sleeked black hair and a mustache and goatee. People—especially lesser-ranked military personnel—often found the natural intensity of his features intimidating.

The newcomer who walked toward him across the wide, glossy-floored concourse, smiling in greeting, looked superficially like Fuseli himself. A fit and good-looking man in his early forties perhaps, with prematurely silvering dark hair and a full if neatly-groomed beard. His charcoal five-piece suit was of the expensive type favored by business executives, but Fuseli already recognized the man as a politician: Rusul Abbas. Abbas was a member of the Earth Colonies network's governing body, the Colonial Congress, who Fuseli knew had risen to that position while still serving as the Head Minister of the one and only colony on Hydra—a tiny moon of the dwarf planet, Pluto.

"Captain Fuseli," Abbas said when the two were close enough to shake hands. "It's a pleasure. Your reputation precedes you."

Fuseli knew that his reputation varied in the eyes of the beholder, as did Abbas's own. In return he said only, "Minister Abbas." He might have called him Congressman Abbas instead, but Fuseli held the belief, based on what he'd heard about the man, that he prioritized the colony on Hydra over his congressional duties. It was this perception, right or wrong, that caused more people than just Fuseli to feel the man's two important positions created a conflict of interest.

"So you recognize me," Abbass said. "Were you told of my coming?"

"No, sir, I wasn't told."

"Ah, well, I'll see that you're filled in about my visit immediately. Your commander, General Stroud, will be joining us remotely."

"Very good," Fuseli said. Stroud was one of the only officers of such rank that Fuseli had ever trusted implicitly, and knowing that his old friend would be present virtually to help explain whatever this was about put him more at ease. Though he still remained guarded. What did this man from Hydra want from him?

"Is there a meeting room nearby we can go to for that?" Abbas asked, glancing around them.

"There is," Fuseli said. "This way." He started walking in the direction of a meeting room that was just off the concourse, in fact. The two details of security personnel—Fuseli's men in arctic camos, and the more formidable-looking black-garbed newcomers—moved with them. Along with the guards and himself Abbas had brought two staff members of one kind or another, both also wearing smart, five-pieces charcoal suits. As they walked, Abbas introduced them.

"I'm sorry; these are two aides of mine. This is Isobel Higgins," he said, indicating a shortish young woman Fuseli judged to be only in her twenties. Her freckled, blue-eyed face was framed in thick curtains of long, coppery hair.. Quite the rare mutation these days, Fuseli thought. He considered the young woman quite pretty, found the prominent ears that poked through her rare red hair oddly charming.

"Ms. Higgins," Fuseli said, reaching across Abbas as they walked to shake her small hand.

"Dr. Fuseli," she said, smiling. He always found it interesting, even revealing, whether people addressed him as a man of medicine or as a military officer.

"Do people call you Belle, or … "

"Izzy," she said.

"That was my next question."

"And this," Abbas went on, indicating the other aide, "is Josef Elmi."

"Mr. Elmi," Fuseli said, extending his hand to him as well.

"Captain," said Elmi, grinning, his large teeth very bright against the young Black man's complexion. Fuseli judged Elmi—tall and thin in build, with a bony face—to be in his early thirties.

Hm, Fuseli thought, taking note. Captain to this one, not Doctor. He often sensed that those who chose to address him as the former were wary of him as a soldier, rather than trusting him as a healer. Sometimes he felt it was only he who saw him as both equally.

"No nicknames for me, unfortunately," Elmi continued, that bright grin still plastered on.

"Not even Joe?"

"Well, Joe for you if you like."

"Are you two congressional aides?" Fuseli asked. "Or … "

"They're aides of mine from Colony Hydra," Abbas answered for his young staff members.

"I see," said Fuseli. So … was this not congressional business?

"Though, they do occasionally serve double duty," Abbas added.

"Like yourself," Fuseli said.

He saw the congressman's smile flicker a little. No doubt Abbas was sensitive about people's attitudes toward his dual roles. He had received a good amount of criticism for it.

"Here we are," Fuseli said, ushering the party into the meeting room in question.

"Did you come here from Congress," Fuseli asked casually as the party filed into the meeting room and took seats around its long, polished table, "or all the way from Hydra?"

The two groups of security personnel fell into position at the door, flanking it on either side. Though all of them were Colonial Forcers, one might have sensed an invisible hostility between the soldiers, like members of two opposing sports teams in their different uniform colors.

Abbas said, "I had some business here on Earth for a few days, but now that's wrapped up and I'll be returning to Hydra. And I hope you'll be accompanying me."

"Oh?" said Fuseli.

"But I'm getting ahead of myself. Let's call up General Stroud—I know he's been standing by for my arrival."

Abbass tapped at the tiny screen of his wrist comp device, and sent a signal from it to a large vid screen on the meeting room's far wall. While Fuseli watched him do this, Izzy Higgins leaned toward him and asked, "Have you ever been to Hydra before, Dr. Fuseli?"

"I haven't, and since we're all becoming so informal, Izzy," Fuseli told her, "and seeing as how you're not military personnel, you can call me Robert. If you're lucky, you might even call me Bob someday."

The young woman laughed. And while Abbas completed the connection of his wrist comp to the wall screen, he smiled over at Fuseli and said, "Well, since we're all doing it, you can call me Russ."

"Russ it is," said Fuseli, in a tone that masked his unhappiness. Accompany Head Minister Rusul Abbas to that misshapen pebble of rock around Pluto, of all places?

Now the wall screen became filled with a feed of General Aaron Stroud, seated behind his desk in his office at Port Haven station. Port Haven was a massive, double-ringed space station in orbit around Pluto, and the outermost line of defensive for this solar system—and hence for the Earth. That is, along with a substantial military base down on the surface of Pluto itself, with another on its largest moon, Charon, besides.

For his part, Stroud came across like a too good-looking movie star playing the role of some main character's silvery-haired grandfather.

"Good to see you, Bob," Stroud said.

Fuseli leaned toward Izzy and whispered, "See?" Then he straightened up in his chair and said, "Good to see you, too, sir."

"How are you and Rhan making out down there at the South Pole?" A poor choice of words, Fuseli thought. "We're doing okay, sir. Rhan's a bit restless, not loving the isolation here, but ... "

"I hear ya, I hear ya. Hopefully we'll be sending her to some more inviting spot soon enough. In the meantime, there's a less than inviting spot I need to send *you* to, Bob."

"And that's Hydra?"

"Yes. So Congressman Abbas, here, has filled you in?" On the screen, Stroud nodded politely toward Abbas.

"No more than that, sir."

Stroud grunted. "Okay, Bob, so what it is, is ... well, Congressman Abbas will explain the particulars to you in more detail than I can. But the short of it is, I'm sure you're aware of the implants the Hydran colonists all share. Congressman Abbas included."

Since the arrival of Abbas's party at the research base, Fuseli had tried not to make it obvious that he was stealing peeks at their implants. It wasn't just Isobel Higgin's cute ears that poked out from her fiery hair. Clamped to the back of her head—and the back of the heads of both Abbas himself and the other aide, Josef Elmi—was a round metal cap, iridescent green in color, without any visible keys or other controls, just a few seams almost like the sutures in a skull, and one small indicator light on the lower edge that glowed a steady amber. Fuseli knew these green metal caps, surgically affixed directly to the skull, were referred to by the colonists of Hydra as Mergers.

That was the term Fuseli used now, to show he understood what his commanding officer referred to. "Mergers."

"Yes. Well, in recent weeks it appears that a virus has been introduced into the Merger units, that's negatively effecting a growing number of Hydrans … "

Fuseli cut off Stroud by swiveling to face Abbas. "Could this be a terrorist attack?"

"That's certainly a consideration," Abbas said grimly. "Determining the cause of this virus is part of the reason we need your help as a medical officer, Captain Fuseli. You have a wide range of experiences, even with alien races. And General Stroud says you're currently between assignments."

"More or less," Fuseli said, resisting the urge to object that he'd been assisting the researchers at Base Amundsen-Scott in studying that fascinating anomaly, Rhan Luyen. He knew he was more along for the ride than anything, mainly serving as a familiar face to keep their subject comfortable, and keep her protected. Not to mention, he'd been using his time at the Antarctica base to more fully recover from serious wounds he'd received during his mission to Titania. But if Stroud was assigning him to look into the problems at Colony Hydra, how much could he protest, in a profession where orders were orders? Nevertheless, he did object somewhat by saying, "But I'm more familiar with organic viruses, Minister Abbas … not so much technological viruses."

"We haven't established whether this apparent virus is biological or technological," Abbas said. "It could be a bio-weapon, a contamination or infection, or simply a flaw in our technology. We're having another expert assigned to Hydra, in addition to yourself, to investigate the technological angle. Since that individual's regular post is on Port Haven, he'll already be waiting on Hydra for us when we get there, commencing his investigation."

"I see," said Fuseli. "So what are the symptoms of this virus or malfunction or whatever it is?"

Abbas began to explain, and despite his reservations Fuseli had to admit the situation sounded serious … especially since the colonists on Hydra included children.

- 3 -

Fuseli made sure to tell Rhan what Abbas had reported to him, about the awfulness being experienced by certain colonists on Hydra, and the anxiety it brought about in their (as yet) unaffected friends and loved ones. He hoped this would demonstrate to her why he had to go there, in addition to the simple fact that he had been ordered to do so. She seemed genuinely disturbed by what he told her, and being a mother—her teenaged daughter in the custody of her ex-husband, back on that alternate Earth, wherever that was—she was especially concerned about the welfare of the children of the Hydra colony. And yet …

"But why does it have to be *you* to go?"

Fuseli sighed sympathetically. They sat together on the edge of her bed, in her quarters, the door of which was never kept locked at night. From the start, after Rhan's virtual imprisonment at the Titania research base, he had insisted that she never be confined like that here. Then again, where was she going to escape to, outside on that expanse of ice? Would he have insisted the same if she were being held at a base in a less inhospitable place?

He replied, "It's like they said … I'm between assignments. I know, I know … but that's how they see it. They see me as more of a helpful outsider here at this base, when it comes to you."

"Well, I might just turn out to be less cooperative with these people if you're not around."

"Please, Rhan, don't be like that. Stay on their good side, and you'll be trusted more and more, and one day soon I hope they will let you integrate into society somewhere, like any regular person. Look … I hope this won't take too long, and I'll get back to your side whether you're here or somewhere else just as soon as I can."

"Until the next mission they call you away on."

"True. But I'll always be with you, as long as you want that, in-between those missions."

Rhan looked down at her hands, knotted together in her lap like two puzzle pieces that didn't quite fit. "I know I'm being selfish. You're a doctor. People need you."

"I'm being selfish, too, because I really don't want to go. And I have personal reasons for that—beyond you, even."

Rhan looked back up at him. "Reasons like what?"

"The Hydrans themselves," he admitted. "They're a cult, Rhan. I'm not saying there aren't very interesting aspects to what they delve into. It's just ... I'd rather see those people explore what they're learning purely as researchers, as scientists, instead of as *believers*. As in ... cultists. Especially where surgical procedures are part of it all. And where children are involved, and subjected to the same poorly understood experiences the adults undergo."

"It does sound dangerous. Reckless and risky."

"Precisely."

"Have you told your friend Stroud about your reservations?"

"I will, for all the good it will do. Not only do I have to follow his command, but with Abbas being a member of Congress, I don't need him putting heat on me from that corner. I've made enough enemies in my career as it is, which is why I don't ever see myself becoming more than a captain."

"I understand, Robert. I do."

"But you don't have to like it."

"I sure don't."

"All reservations about the Hydrans' beliefs aside, and about what they subject their kids to ... what they're experiencing now with these malfunctions *has* to be stopped before it spreads. So, I hope you don't think that I'm being weak by not putting up a fight."

Rhan smiled, and started undoing the front of her top. "You want to prove to me one last time, before you go, just how strong you are?"

Fuseli smiled, watching the fabric part open to reveal the warm, golden-hued flesh within. "Of course. Purely in the interest of science, you understand."

Part Three

The Lancet

- 1 -

With approximately three billion miles to cover from Earth to Pluto, it was going to take over ten days of space travel to reach the moon called Hydra.

At least, those ten days would be spent aboard a large hospital vessel, the Earth Colonies Ship Lancet, with plenty of room to move around. The E.C.S. Lancet had been scheduled to deliver fresh personnel from Earth to Port Haven space station anyway, to cycle out some of the medical staff there, and from Port Haven it would then be a short jump to the Plutonian moon named Hydra. Fuseli hadn't been on a hospital vessel of this size since he'd commanded the ill-fated E.C.S. Caduceus, but this vessel was much newer than that refurbished military ship, and Fuseli was impressed with it. Touring its facilities and chatting up its crew—particularly medical staff, of course—would help him pass the time, though he couldn't help but harbor a touch of sourness that he would most likely never be handed command of such a craft. Well, he told himself, maybe if this business on Hydra went well his fortunes might change. After all, it couldn't hurt to get in the good graces of a member of the Colonial Congress.

"Gotta be more cooperative," he said to himself aloud on the first day out, alone in his quarters and contemplating himself in the bathroom's vidscreen. "Like I always preach to Rhan. Less ruffling of feathers. Less complaining about shitty missions. Oops ... did I say that?"

He debated calling Stroud and voicing his misgivings about the strange beliefs of the Hydrans, but decided he'd do that in person when they reached Port Haven. What he did do, though, at the start of day two, was ask Rusul Abbas what kind of medical team they had at Colony Hydra, and who it was best to confer with regarding the situation they were experiencing there.

Sitting across from Fuseli in the Lancet's mess hall, over Fuseli's morning coffee and the congressman's tea, Abbas replied, "Unfortunately, our medical staff is quite limited. But owing to the proximity of Port Haven, whenever we have a serious accident or such, we either ship the individual over there or else some med people from Port Haven will pay a house call to Hydra."

"But you must have someone there in charge of medical matters," Fuseli said. "What I mean to ask is, who oversees the implanting of those Merger devices into your colonists? Who maintains them?"

"Well," Abbas said, shifting his weight in his chair and glancing off toward the cafeteria line with what seemed to be a touch of discomfort, "two different groups are involved with the Mergers. There's our amazing tech department, that helped develop them in the first place and maintains what little needs to be maintained. That is, what little needed to be maintained before the present circumstances. And then, as I say, there's our humble med team."

"Run by?" Fuseli pressed.

Abbas turned to face Fuseli again, and told him the name of the medical team's chief. As it turned out, the medical team boiled down to mostly a one-man show. Except that its chief wasn't just not a man ... it wasn't even human.

Fuseli made the call in his quarters, sitting at a little flip-down desk with his wrist comp projecting a larger, holographic screen that floated in the air before him. Abbas had called ahead to prepare the med chief for Fuseli's vid call, and even though Fuseli knew what he was going to see he still didn't care for it.

"A pleasure to, ah, speak with you, Dr. Fuseli," said the robot.

Fuseli drew a long breath through his nose, then quipped, "Can you put the med chief on, are am I speaking to … it?"

"I'm the, uh, the head of the medical team at Colony Hydra, Dr. Fuseli." The robot spoke with the voice of a young human woman. If Fuseli's eyes had been closed, he would easily have been fooled, but his eyes told him the real story. This automaton seated at a desk, presumably in the colony's medical center, only resembled a human being in having a head and two arms attached to a torso, and perhaps two legs below the limits of the frame. The arms were silvery and fully segmented along their length, but the hands, torso, and head were all of an emerald green metal that gave off an oily iridescence with the shifting of light. Its face was nothing but a flat silver oval set in the front of that metallic green skull. The robot went on, "You can, ah, call me Florence."

"Stop it," Fuseli said.

"Doctor?"

"Quit it with the affected stammering. Just speak plainly."

The robot hesitated, and when it spoke again the quirky pauses in its speech were gone. "I'm sorry, Doctor; it's a programmed effect to make me sound more natural to my fellow colonists."

Fellow colonists? "Well, the effect is hardly natural, when I'm talking to a faceless robot."

"Would this help, then?" Suddenly a human face filled that oval in the front of the robot's head: that of an attractive woman with Asian features. For a second Fuseli was almost startled, thinking the robot had somehow reached into his mind for an image of Rhan, but that was a silly thought. The woman portrayed on the robot's screen was probably ten years younger than Rhan's forty-one, and very likely not based on a living woman anyway, however lifelike.

"Definitely not," Fuseli said. "Only more annoying."

"I apologize, Doctor." In a blink, the Asian woman's face vanished, replaced by that empty silver oval. "I'm only trying to make you feel more comfortable with me."

"I'll feel more comfortable when I better understand the nature of the problem the colonists are experiencing there on Hydra," Fuseli said. "Though, I'm assuming you can't tell me much more than Minister Abbas has already, or else I wouldn't be on my way over there right now."

"That's correct, Dr. Fuseli," said the robot called Florence. "I've run diagnostics on the Merger devices here—both unaffected units, and those that seemed to have malfunctioned—and as yet I haven't determined the cause of the problems we've been facing. I look forward to your arrival, and that of Mr. Zarate. I have faith that in working together, the two of you can isolate and help us address the source of this terrible occurrence."

Marco Zarate was the special diagnostic technician who would be arriving at Colony Hydra from Port Haven any time now, and have a crack at the problem before Fuseli arrived. Zarate had been advised, though, not to meddle with any Merger device currently implanted in a living host until Fuseli got there. Zarate would have to be content with those units retrieved from, thus far, four dead Hydrans.

"Who is it that implants the Merger devices in the colonists?" Fuseli asked the robot.

"I handle that procedure myself, Dr. Fuseli. I'll be happy to show you the equipment with which it's accomplished, once you're here."

"And who trained you to do it? Who developed this process?"

"Ah, so you haven't had a chance to research the origins of our community?"

"I have, a bit, but things have been rushed, as I'm sure you understand. Anyway, I prefer my information straight from the robot's mouth. If you had a mouth."

"Well, that individual would of course be the founder of Colony Hydra," said Florence, its voice conveying a human-sounding sense of pride. "The person whose research led to communication with—or rather, *communion* with—the distant sentient race we call the Nought. None other than the late and sorely missed—"

Before Florence could finish, a Klaxon began sounding loudly through the length and breadth of hospital ship Lancet. Instantly Fuseli was bolting up from his chair.

"What is that siren, Doctor?" asked the robot, its voice sounding genuinely concerned.

"An emergency of some kind," Fuseli said grimly. "Gotta go." Then he cut the call, and headed for the door.

Even as Fuseli entered the corridor beyond his quarters, a new call came over his wrist comp … this one from the Lancet's security chief, whose name was Val Okoro.

On his device's little screen, the Black woman's face was deadly serious. "Captain Fuseli," Okoro said, "please report to Surgical Bay Twelve. There's an emergency."

"What nature?" Fuseli said, as he began racing down the corridor, mindful of direction screens on the walls. He was still orienting himself to the ship, it being only the second day into their journey.

"It's one of the Hydrans, sir," said the security chief. "That thing on his head … "

"Is it Abbas?" Fuseli cut her off, coming to a T at the end of that corridor and taking a right.

"No, sir. His name is Elmi."

- 2 -

The Lancet was six hundred feet long, so there was a lot of ground to cover from bow to stern, but thankfully Fuseli didn't have too far to run from the living quarters to the surgical bays that dominated the vessel at midship. As he entered the corridor along which the bays were arranged, facing each other, he saw a group of people clustered around the closed double doors to Surgical Bay Twelve. Among them were a few members of the ship's medical staff, and five of the Lancet's security people, including chief Val Okoro. She cradled a medical-white Drang assault engine, her four teammates in their white uniforms gripping handguns. In contrast were Rusul Abbas's four black-garbed, helmeted bodyguards with their matching black Drangs, also there outside the surgical bay doors, as was Abbas himself, watching Fuseli's approach. Even from down the corridor, it was plain to see the distress in the man's face.

"Get that robot on your wrist comp again," Fuseli told the Hydran Head Minister as he covered the last feet between them. "Ask it how we can get that implant off Elmi without killing him."

"That can't be done, Captain Fuseli," Abbas said.

"Has anyone even *tried* removing these things when they go haywire?"

"Of course we have! As you know, Captain, four of my people have died on Hydra. If Florence could have removed their Mergers to save them, she would have. Thus far, when one of the Mergers malfunctions in this way it's a death sentence."

"Let me go in there to take a look for myself."

"Captain," Abbas said, "you don't understand! I don't recommend—"

A thud against the sealed double doors, loud enough to be heard through their sturdiness, caused every head to turn toward the sound. A face had appeared in one of the doors' twin windows. Josef Elmi's eyes bulged so wide in his skull that they seemed on the verge of popping straight out of their sockets. Fuseli saw large vein-like structures radiating from the Merger affixed at the back of his head to branch out across his face; veins that didn't fully correspond to typical human anatomy. The largest of them could even be seen throbbing.

Elmi had planted one of his hands on the window, and squashed his face up against it, smearing the lips of his gaping mouth, seemingly straining to release a wail that wouldn't come. Only a muffled, deep and liquid gurgling. He pounded the flat of his hand against the window several times.

"Oh, Josef," Abbas said, already mourning him.

Fuseli pushed his way between the two team of security people to get closer to the doors. "Open it," he said to no one in particular.

"Captain, you can't!" Abbas insisted.

Fuseli snapped his eyes to the those of Security Chief Okoro. "Open it!"

The security chief turned toward the wall controls for the doors, a red light on the panel indicating that someone had locked Elmi inside. She reached out, but hesitated with her finger only a few atoms away from depressing the key to unlock the doors.

"Wait!" Abbas cried, lunging for her.

Then, Elmi changed.

The man had taken a step back from that half of the double doors, and then blood splattered across its window explosively, immediately running down in streams. Through the obscuring gore, however, Fuseli saw that Josef Elmi's face had split open down the center from top to bottom, as if a zipper had been yanked open. Even as this happened, the two halves of flesh were pushed or pulled aside as new structures, rapidly formed, thrust themselves through exposed subcutaneous tissues.

"What is it?" Fuseli heard a young woman cry out behind him, as she entered the corridor. "What's going on?"

Fuseli recognized the voice as belonging to Abbas's other aide, Isobel Higgins, but he didn't turn around to look. He was too mesmerized by what he was seeing—horrified and yet, as a surgeon, fascinated. It was he himself, now, who shot out a hand to Security Chief Okoro to snatch her wrist and prevent her from unlocking the doors. As Abbas had said, it was indeed too late for the man, so he might as well observe the process.

A large, bony orb was what had mostly forced apart the halves of Elmi's face. It was as if his skull were a balloon, and had suddenly been filled with air or liquid or who knew what until it had bulged significantly beyond its natural size. Even more strangely, however, the bared surface of bone appeared to be engraved with countless tiny hexagons, giving it a pebbled effect, though the blood smeared across the glistening orb and the quickness of events made it hard to be sure. More certain, however, was that Elmi's upper and lower jaws had also broken into halves, and extended out from the ruined face: both the maxilla and the mandible, spreading wide like the double jaws of some gigantic beetle. The four arms of this new mouth, still lined with human teeth, opened and closed convulsively as if in an attempt to grasp on to something … or futilely form words.

Meanwhile, the tongue flopped free from the aide's ruined face, lolling uselessly in front of his neck, and his eyes stared blindly from the folds of flesh bunched at the sides of his head.

"Is it Josef?" Fuseli heard Izzy cry.

"Keep her back!" Fuseli shouted.

He hadn't been shown any vid recordings of this type of occurrence, only limited images of the messy aftermath once the victims were already dead, so he wasn't entirely unprepared for what he saw … but it was one thing to see still images and another to watch it happen so abruptly, so shockingly before your own eyes.

"Is Sandy still in there with him?" he heard one of the med technicians frantically ask another.

Fuseli pushed a security member out of his way to address this woman. "Someone's in there with him?"

Her face a portrait of terror, the med tech said, "I think so! The man came into surgery looking for help, holding onto his head. We rushed him into the nearest bay, but then he went into these terrible convulsions—lashing out at us, with crazy eyes, like he wanted to kill us—so we hurried out here to call for help." The young tech fought back sobs. "I'm sorry, but we were afraid … we didn't know what to do! Then after we locked him in, we realized Sandy was still in there with him … unless she got out one of the doors into the other bays."

"We'll check," Okoro said. She pointed to two of her security staff in turn. "Bay Ten! Bay Fourteen!"

As the security members bolted for the surgical suites adjoining Bay Twelve on either side, Fuseli returned his attention to the blood-splashed window to see that Elmi had staggered backwards, away from the doors. Now more of the man's body was revealed, although any other alterations to it were no doubt hidden by Elmi's blood-soaked clothing. More pressingly at that moment, Fuseli saw the aide turn sharply toward a sound behind him—no doubt a sob or whimper. It was then that through the doors' twin windows, those in the corridor spotted another young med tech crouching behind an examination table, trying in vain to make herself into a small unnoticeable ball. Fuseli saw that blood ran from her nostrils, likely from a broken nose.

Upon noticing her there, Elmi lunged for the med tech … and even in the corridor they heard her scream.

"Is he trying to hurt her?" Fuseli heard Okoro shout to Abbas.

"Yes," Abbas said in a dead-sounding voice.

Fuseli himself punched the key to unlock and open the doors to Surgical Bay Twelve, and even as the panels slid back and he plunged inside, the doors on either side of the room—there to expand the work area if the need arose, or as secondary exits in the case of fire or other calamity—slid open as well, and Okoro's two people surged in, both with handguns ready. Fuseli drew his own Scythe .55 sidearm from the holster at his hip.

"Josef!" he yelled.

Elmi was hunched over, reaching out to the tech with both hands as she tried to tuck herself into an even smaller ball, but at Fuseli's exclamation the aide whirled around to face him … if his head could now be said to have a face.

"Josef," Fuseli said, "let us help you!" He knew there was no help to be had for the man, but what he didn't know was whether Elmi could be communicated with in this state.

The discarded eyes on the sides of his head were glassy and unseeing, but that bulging skull orb lowered toward Fuseli as if somehow it *perceived* him. The long tongue swung free, dripping saliva, the four new mouthparts opened and closed, and there came a choking gurgle like that of a man with his throat cut—and as a seasoned veteran of the bloody Gurm Conflict, Fuseli knew that sound—but no words were forthcoming. And then Elmi raised his hands and came rushing at Fuseli. Fuseli just had time enough to note that the hands flopped uselessly from their wrists, broken off but hanging by strips of of flesh. The ends of the radius and ulna protruded from the meat, and in either arm these bones opened and closed independently of each other, in the uncanny way the man's jaws moved. Bones and muscles, both, had been repurposed.

In that moment, Fuseli the surgeon noticed that the natural nub, called the styloid process, at the end of the radius and ulna bones in both arms looked oddly curved and decidedly more pointed than normal. Like the tarsal claw of an insect.

Before the aide could strike or seize Fuseli with these weirdly reconfigured limbs, he extended his Scythe and fired once into the man's chest, where he hoped that at least the heart remained in its regular position. In another situation he might have shot his opponent in the head, but even at that moment Fuseli was thinking of preserving Elmi as best he could as a specimen for study. He was interested in that head, especially with the Merger device still clamped to the back of it.

As the projectile plowed into him Elmi jolted and emitted a louder, wetter gurgle. A gout of blood shot from his mouth, striking Fuseli's shoes. And yet, the man took another staggering step forward. With Fuseli having already discharged his gun, the two guards who'd entered the room with him pointed their own weapons, but hesitated for fear of striking the captain. It didn't matter; Fuseli fired the Scythe again twice in rapid succession. Peripherally, he was aware of exclamations of horror from those gathered in the corridor behind him.

This time Elmi dropped, his transfigured skull striking the floor hard. It didn't pop like a balloon instead sounded quite firm. After several violent electrified spasms, the body finally realized it was dead and went still.

At that, the tech named Sandy rose sobbing from behind the examination table and others surged into the room. Fuseli turned toward them, his eyes seeking out the med tech he had spoken with.

"Get his body thoroughly scanned, then place it into a cryo chamber for preservation."

At least now he had something to occupy himself with, in the eight full days remaining before the Lancet arrived at Port Haven.

"Yes, Doctor," the woman said, but first she rushed past Fuseli—stepping around the strange corpse in its growing pond of blood—to see to Sandy, who'd suffered a blow from Elmi when the techs had tried to care for him.

Fuseli saw Abbas there in the open doorway, and Izzy behind him, barefoot and wearing a t-shirt and sweatpants, perhaps having woken from a nap. Tears filled her eyes, a hand pressed to her mouth.

"There was no choice, Captain," Abbas said, wagging his head. "I understand. Now you see just how critical this matter is. Poor Josef … but that could just as easily have been me. Or Izzy."

Fuseli didn't need this man to exonerate him for shooting Elmi. Coldly he said, "We have some things to discuss, Minister Abbas."

- 3 -

"These alterations aren't random," Fuseli said, pointing out features of a recorded scan of Elmi's body, on a holographic screen that hovered in the air before the two men in a meeting room Abbas had opened for them. He motioned with his hand to zoom in on the view of the dead man's head. "The same characteristics appear in the images you've shown me of the four previous victims. The change to the maxilla and mandible … the hands detaching, and arm bones exposed. And these markings on the skull … "

"Precisely," Abbas said. "The mutations are always the same."

Fuseli pointed at the Merger, which in this scan filter appeared only as a mysterious dark blob. "The question is, *why* do these certain changes take place? But I have a question for *you*, sir." He swiveled toward Abbas. "Well … one of many, to start with."

"Yes, Captain?"

"Why haven't I been shown any vids of these occurrences … only still images? You can't tell me that your colony doesn't have security cameras."

"We do, of course, Captain." Abbas hesitated, holding Fuseli's intense gaze, and finally went on, "Due to the misconceptions of many members of the public, and even outright persecution—the very things that decided us to create our own colony on Hydra in the first place—we've become very protective of our community. Therefore, no video or audio recordings of the Merge ceremony, or anything related to it, are permitted to be shared with the outside world."

"Even with me ... the man you've called in to help you? I mean, I'm going to be seeing this ... *ceremony* of yours myself in person, aren't I?"

Abbas didn't answer.

Fuseli widened his eyes. "*Aren't* I?"

"I'm not sure you need to witness the ceremony itself, Captain Fuseli. You will of course be permitted to examine the Merger devices, both those implanted in living colonists and those retrieved from the dead ... and Florence will show you the equipment with which the units are implanted. But ... the ceremony ... "

"Only for the initiated, huh?"

"I'm afraid so."

Fuseli sighed, "Jesus." He bit back his words. He was speaking with a member of the Colonial Congress, and the Head Minister of Hydra's only colony besides, and he knew General Stroud would expect nothing but professionalism and respect from him. Still, Stroud knew him better than anybody, and if he let loose his own feelings every now and then his commander shouldn't be surprised.

Still, Fuseli changed the topic for now, and again pointed out a feature on the hologram. This time he specifically indicated where the entirety of the frontal bone, all the way back to the coronal suture, had not only enlarged dramatically but manifested those odd interlinked patterns. He zoomed in on them, where in close-up their geometric perfection was even more striking. "Do you know what these remind me of, Minister?"

"What is that?"

"Maybe you could tell me. Maybe you know more about these physical alterations than you're comfortable sharing."

"Please, Captain, just say what you're thinking."

"What I'm thinking is, these intricate raised patterns that formed on Elmi's skull put me in mind of the ommatidia of an insect's compound eye. Each unit having its own lens to detect light and color."

"Well Captain, clearly the material of Josef's skull didn't form such lenses. Unless that's what you're leading up to."

"It didn't, but ... it looks like it was *trying* to."

"Don't patterns like this appear elsewhere in nature, spontaneously?"

"They do. On a turtle's shell ... in tripe ... in the honeycomb of bees. Rock formations called columnar jointing. Hell, the north pole of Saturn has a hexagonal shape." Fuseli went quiet, studying the enlarged image of Josef Elmi's frontal bone. In a distant tone, as if now only talking to himself, he went on, "But what I should be focusing on more is better understanding the changes that took place to his brain."

"Are those changes severe?" Abbas asked.

"They're ... not as severe as one might think, at least from looking at the scans so far, but his brain is surely showing anomalies. The question is, are these anomalies already present in the brains of *all* you colonists who've had a Merger implanted? On Hydra, I'm going to want to scan all of you for comparison." Fuseli faced Abbas again. "How many colonists are there, again?"

"We're a sizable community, for such a tiny moon," Abbas said, rather proudly. "You can endeavor to scan all of us, Captain, but there are nine hundred and fifty-three of us who live on Hydra, plus another couple dozen who regularly go forth to other worlds and space stations to pursue business of various types abroad. Our numbers are growing all the time ... and yet our colony is only seven years old."

"Yeah, sounds like I'll be taking a sampling of your community, then." Fuseli mused again, then said, "Can I at least, for now, ask you a little about the process you call Merging?"

"You may ask," Abbas said guardedly.

"At this ceremony, does the entirety of the colony participate? In groups, or all at once?"

"The Ceremony Chamber can accommodate roughly a hundred individuals, so we take assigned shifts. The process varies in duration … it depends on the strength of our connection with the Nought. In the beginning, some days we weren't able to make a connection at all, but with the improvement over the years of the Merger units we've more regularly been able to intercept and maintain a strong connection."

"Do you ever pursue this connection individually, outside of the ceremony?"

"Yes," said Abbas, "and I'm sure that was what Josef was doing, alone in his quarters, at the time his Merger apparently malfunctioned. The malfunctions only seems to occur during the Merge."

"Hm." Fuseli nodded, digesting this. "I don't know how that implant could be producing these radical body changes … but then I still don't know anything about those contraptions at all."

"I'm not a technical person," Abbas said. "You'll best be served by discussing the Merger units themselves with Florence."

"And this Marco Zarate guy," Fuseli said, "when he gets a look at those things. In the meantime, Minister, I can't stress enough that you and your aide Isobel should not attempt that Merge procedure. In fact, you should tell all the colonists on Hydra to refrain from that ceremony of yours until our investigation is concluded."

Abbas shifted in his seat uneasily, and even before he spoke Fuseli knew what he was going to say. "Captain, the Merge is simply too important to us to refrain from. It forms the very *center* of our lives, don't you see? It's why we've all chosen this challenging life on that hostile little rock."

"It's so important that you'd risk your lives rather than give it up, if only for a short time?"

Abbas smiled. "Captain Fuseli, you're a soldier. Haven't you risked your life for things that mattered to you, such as the safety of your fellow soldiers, and that of the innocent people you defended, rather than *refrain* from such risks?"

"I'm not sure that's a good comparison. Maybe I'd understand how important this is to you if I had a religion."

"Our way is not a religion."

"If you say so," Fuseli said.

- 4 -

"Were you and Josef close?" Fuseli asked.

Izzy Higgins lay on her back on a narrow table inside a clear cylinder as her body was scanned from her small feet in their white ankle socks to the top of her copper-haired head. She wore black tights and a gray t-shirt with the logo of Colony Hydra on the front. It portrayed a stylized image of a giant satellite dish against a starry black sky.

It was the third day, by terrestrial reckoning, of their voyage from Earth to Port Haven station in orbit around Pluto.

"Not close-close," Izzy replied, staring up stiffly as the scan beam washed over her. "But we were friends."

Several technicians were assisting Fuseli here in one of the imaging rooms. He was glad none of them were robots. The proportion of robot workers to human workers in any field was restricted by law, lest humans find it more difficult to find employment than it already was in a greatly automated society. Plus, he just preferred to interact with humans, for all their flaws, knowing he wasn't free of flaws himself. He wasn't keen on the medical department on Hydra—inadequate as it seemed to the needs of almost a thousand colonists—being overseen by a stammering machine.

"That'll do," Fuseli said. A beep announced the scan was completed, and the cover of the cylinder slid open. He stepped closer to offer Izzy a hand as she sat up on the table's edge. She took it with a grateful smile. He stooped down to retrieve her shoes and handed them to her.

"Did you see anything strange?" she asked.

"That beautiful red hair is quite anomalous these days."

She gave him a look. "Besides that?"

"That odd green cap obscuring your beautiful red hair." He pointed to the back of her head. "I don't suppose I could talk you into refraining from the Merge until I find out what's going on?"

"Captain," she sighed. "Minister Abbas told me you'd suggested that. I just can't. I know you don't understand."

"I don't." Fuseli nodded his thanks to the techs who'd assisted him. "I'll go over these scans later," he told Izzy, "but just now I didn't pick up anything *too* unusual."

"Not *too*? How about somewhat unusual?"

"The brain scan flagged you for slight abnormality of Broca's area in the frontal lobe."

"Which does what?"

"Language processing. Also in the inferior frontal gyrus. Again, used in language processing. These might be the centers receiving the signals the Nought transmit, or broadcast, or whatever they do. I'll also have to look into any response patterns of mirror neurons."

"Which are?"

"A neural process that can make telepathy possible."

"Oh … wow! Has anyone ever tried to boost that, to make it more possible?"

"It's been achieved, but the science is suppressed. Think of the adverse effects telepathy would have on society. Would you want to have no privacy whatsoever, from family, friends, and strangers … and especially from the government?"

"Yeah, that would be a horrible way to live … people inside your head all the time."

Fuseli arched an eyebrow at her. "Exactly."

Izzy smiled. "That's not the same thing as what we experience with the Nought, Captain."

"Robert."

"Robert," she amended. "Or is it Bob?"

"I hereby grant you permission to use Bob. So, since we're both free at the moment would you be interested in joining me for a coffee in the mess hall?"

"A tea perhaps."

Fuseli groaned. "Ah, you sad tea people."

So it was that Fuseli's black coffee and Izzy's green tea steamed before them, and they resumed their conversation.

"Even minor changes to your brain structure is concerning to me," Fuseli was telling her. "I hate to alarm you, but I need to. I'm eager to know if I'll see this in others."

"I'm sure Minister Abbas would consent to a scan."

"But you know what I mean? This could be the start of far greater changes to come … the first sign of whatever process triggered Elmi's body to react in the way it did."

"It is frightening to think of," Izzy murmured, suddenly warming her hands on the outside of her mug.

"We were talking about receiving these transmissions or such from the Nought. I don't understand much about that, and no one does … thanks to the secrecy of your community."

"It's just that we faced mistrust and abuse, at first, when we lived amongst others. Only those who submitted to the Merger implant and experienced the Merge for themselves could possibly understand. Other people said we were being brainwashed or manipulated by a hostile alien force that was trying to spy on us. Or they thought we were just zombies without minds of our own. But when we formed that community on Hydra, of only others like us, then we found the peace and total acceptance we needed and deserve."

"Have you been with the colony from its inception?"

"No, I myself have only been there two years."

"Are your parents Hydrans?"

Izzy lowered her gaze to the tendrils of steam coming off her tea. "They're divorced. My mother lives on Port Haven; I hope I don't run into her when we stop off there to grab our shuttle to Hydra. My father lives in Punktown."

"Yuck," said Fuseli.

"Both of them have disowned me, pretty much, for joining the Hydrans. They definitely don't understand what we experience through the Merge."

"And getting back to that ... what does it feel like, when you're communing with the Nought?"

Izzy lifted her eyes again and their brightness returned. "It's beautiful, Robert. I mean ... Bob. Part of the reason we don't talk about it with outsiders is because it's so indescribable."

"So it's a transporting experience, seeing things from the point of view of a nonhuman race?"

"It isn't quite like that. It isn't about seeing, but about feeling ... and it almost isn't even about feeling so much as *not* feeling. Not feeling anything."

"Hence ... the Nought. Is that a name you Hydrans gave them, or a translation, so to speak, of the name they know themselves by?"

"It's our own name. We don't get language from them. That is to say, they don't talk to us. We just link our minds with them and share what they experience as they commune with each other."

Fuseli sipped his coffee thoughtfully. "I hate to say it, but because no one has any truly empirical evidence of this distant alien race, there are those who dispute their very existence. Those who say you people are deceiving us ... or even deceiving yourselves. Convincing yourselves."

"I know people say those things. My mother says things like that."

"It's just that no one has said exactly where these Nought are supposed to be. Do you Hydrans even know?"

"Not to my knowledge. We only know that they're beyond the reach of all communications systems but the one devised by Klaus Gaithersburg himself."

"Ah yes, the great entrepreneur Klaus Gaithersburg," Fuseli said. "Your Dr. Florence started to tell me about him. He's just about as mysterious as the Nought themselves. Did you ever meet him? Ah, but that was before your time, wasn't it?"

"Yes, he died four years ago, on Hydra."

"What did he die of?"

"He was rather old. Eighty-six, I believe. He suffered from a number of ailments."

"I see. So he detected the transmissions of the Nought, and eventually designed a system that could contact them through mental activity."

"Well, yeah, kind of … but we don't really *contact* each other, like I said. They don't even really transmit or broadcast, like you're saying. It's more like, uh, emissions … emanations. Mr. Gaithersburg picked up this mental activity while scanning distant regions of space. They didn't reach out to us, and probably weren't even aware of us until Mr. Gaithersburg was able to reach out to their minds with his own mental activity. Even then it wasn't a conversation, but a communion. And it was while experiencing that amazing communion that he shared in their own Merge, as he came to call it. It's something beautiful they had for themselves, and now we can benefit from it, too."

"The indescribable bliss of the Merge."

Izzy looked a tad hurt. "You're mocking me. All of us."

"No, no, Izzy." He reached across and rested his hand atop one of hers. "Like I said, I still have a lot to learn about all this. I really need to get to Hydra and see more for myself."

"Don't you think you're a little too old to be courting Izzy, Captain Fuseli?" said an approaching voice.

Fuseli turned around in his seat and saw a smiling Rusul Abbas coming their way, carrying his own tea. Unlike Izzy, who had taken to wearing less formal attire on their journey, he looked as sharp as ever in his five-piece charcoal business suit. Uninvited, he took a spare chair at their table.

Izzy looked embarrassed, withdrawing her hand from under Fuseli's, and Fuseli's eyes on Abbas turned steely. "I'm in a relationship with a woman back home, Minister Abbas."

"Yes, so I heard—that woman from an alternate Earth, apparently. What a fascinating situation. I looked into your background when General Stroud suggested you for this situation. You have an impressive, if sometimes tragic history. Medic in that horrific Gurm Conflict. A prisoner of war during the conflict with the Cepha race. The sad fate of your ship the Caduceus … "

"Life's not a bowl of cherries." Fuseli took in the blank expressions of the two Hydrans. "It's an archaic expression. Another archaic expression is *playing Russian roulette*. It's when you take a dangerous chance, like putting a single bullet in the cylinder of a revolver and pressing it to your fragile skull."

"A revolver?" Izzy said.

"Never mind. I think my general point is clear enough."

"I do appreciate your concern for us," Abbas said. "I'm sure that concern will serve you well in your investigation on Hydra. Oh, and Captain. I'm sorry—I was only teasing you about flirting with Izzy, here."

"Nothing wrong with a little flirting, is there?" Fuseli drained the last of his coffee and stood up. "Well, thank you for our date, Izzy, but I guess I'll get back to imaging and see what else I might learn from your scan … especially when I compare it to the scan of Josef Elmi's brain. If you'll excuse me."

As Fuseli started away, he saw Rusul Abbas and Izzy Higgins exchange a look with each other. Full of secrets, those two, thought Fuseli.

- 5 -

Tomorrow they would reach Port Haven. By the reckoning of time on

Earth, that is. Space itself had no awareness of, let alone concern about, time.

Fuseli had spent part of the trip delving deeper into the brain scans of Josef Elmi, whose body remained in a cryo chamber with the Merger still affixed to his misshapen skull. His wish was to watch the robot called Florence remove it, so he could better understand that process.

He had also scanned the brain of Rusul Abbas, and found the same subtle but concerning anomalies he had seen in Izzy. Had either of them Merged in the past nine days, but not made him aware of it? He'd asked the two Hydrans this, but both had evaded the question, which led him to believe they had … much to his frustration.

Besides killing more time by enjoying further coffee dates with Izzy, who had revealed more details about her fraught family history—including a single miserable visit to her father in the city of Punktown, on the far exoplanet Oasis, shortly before her move to Hydra—Fuseli had returned to chatting with the impressive hospital ship's crew and commanding officer. But he had also studied further the utterly perplexing physiognomy of Josef Elmi. Besides the shocking outward features, such as the transformation of the arms and the bizarre skull patterns, he'd noted that there had been some displacement and deformation of his inner organs, plus other portions of his skeleton.

Most significantly, of course, Fuseli had seen that the areas of the brain the diagnostic computer had flagged in Izzy—the inferior frontal gyrus and Broca's area—showed a greater degree of structural abnormality in Elmi, including an increase in size that was not drastic but still wholly unusual.

He did not, however—as he had thought he might—find any mirror neuron activity in his scans of Izzy and Abbas. Might he only witness such activity if he were to scan them during the Merge? Or did the Merger device take the place of that natural telepathic process … synthesize and magnify it? Surely it must. Anyway, without such a device how could human neurons be thought to mirror those of a presumably nonhuman race?

During one coffee date, Fuseli had asked Izzy—whom he felt more comfortable talking with than Abbas, due to her vulnerability and greater, if not total, openness—if the Hydrans had any idea what the Nought race actually looked like.

"I have no idea," she'd replied. "But who knows … judging from the strength of their communion with each other, they may even have transcended the need for physical bodies."

"So … might they then covet human bodies? And hope to hijack more and more of them?"

"But why *would* they? Why would they give up their state of utter connectedness and peace to hop into our crappy bodies, only to die a horrible death inside us?"

"Maybe these are just the initial experiments, like probes, and the full invasion is yet to come."

Izzy had wagged her head sadly as she raised her green tea for a sip. "Spoken like a true soldier, Bob."

Fuseli and General Stroud had shared a few conversations over the past nine days, also, and Fuseli had filled his commanding officer in on Elmi's transformation, his attempted attacks on himself and others, and the man's subsequent death and virtual autopsy.

"Would he have died eventually anyway, if you hadn't had to kill him?" Stroud asked at one point.

"That's what I've been led to believe. If the alterations continue, the body is so compromised it expires."

"Led to believe? You sound dubious."

"Of course I'm dubious, sir. These people only share when they have to, and then only as little as they can get away with."

"Patience, Bob. I know they're an unusual community. Anyway, look, we'll talk more in person once you're here, and I'll even let you vent some more if you just maintain a nice bedside manner when you're around them."

"That's a big request to make from me," Fuseli said, "but for you I'll try."

Despite his misgivings about a machine being in charge of medical affairs at Colony Hydra, however human-like its AI pretended to be, Fuseli decided to touch base again with Florence before their imminent arrival on that moon. This time the robot knew right away not to use its artificial speech quirks with him.

"Have you had a chance to go over the scans I sent you of Josef Elmi?" he asked.

"Of course, Dr. Fuseli," said Florence, its blank faceplate centered on the comp screen in his quarters. "His deformations are very similar to those found on the four previous victims here on Hydra, though of a somewhat more profound degree."

"Do you think the effects are worsening with each case, then?"

"There might be evidence of that, Doctor."

"I've been comparing the scans myself," Fuseli said, opening a number of other holographic screens in the air and shuffling through them. "For instance, I think I do see an increasing deformity of the ulna and radius bones, in regard to the styloid process. On the first victim, um … Lalita Begum … the styloid process of these four bones appears normal, but chronologically, in each victim thereafter the styloid process grows sharper, until by Josef Elmi we have something like an actual hook."

"Interesting."

"Also, it looks to me like the hexagonal patterns on Begum's skull weren't very defined, while in each subsequent victim they've grown more distinct … though it's hard for me to be sure, based on the limited materials Minister Abbas has seen fit to pass on to me." He said this last with a degree of bitterness even an emotionless robot couldn't miss.

"I believe you're right, Doctor."

"I'm perplexed about the fourth victim." He consulted his list of names again; Fuseli was often too distracted to remember names. "Vardon Grigoryan. I see how the changes to internal organs in victims one through three caused their deaths, especially the ruptured brain aneurysms—which we may have seen in Elmi soon enough had I not had to shoot him."

"Yes, Doctor, he may well have progressed to that state."

"May well have … and yet the funny thing is, while certain deformities have subtly worsened from Begum to Elmi, the severity of damage to internal organs appears to have gradually lessened. As if each victim has been a progression toward something."

"What do you feel this shows a progression toward, if I might ask?"

Fuseli contemplated his floating screens, flicking his gaze from one to another. "Progressing toward a more viable—but less human—being."

"Interesting," Florence said again. "Though, if I may be so frank, that could be a bit of a jump to make at this stage, Doctor."

"I'm only entertaining possibilities. Call it a human's intuition."

"A faculty that I have no doubt serves you well, but if I'm not mistaken you seem to suggest the changes to these victims are intentional … directed … rather than accidents brought about by some flaw either in the Merger system itself or in the human body's relationship to it."

"Again … I'm only throwing ideas out there," Fuseli said. "Getting back to Vardon Grigoryan. Despite what I just said about each victim's organs becoming progressively less fatally altered, despite the increase in certain other deformities, Grigoryan's internal injuries are very traumatic. I'd even go so far to say, Florence, that what I'm seeing in his case—again, based on the limited materials available to me—is that he suffered a gunshot wound. Yet, I'm not seeing that in his inadequate report." Fuseli switched his attention from the secondary screen to the vid screen from which the faceless robot watched him. "Did this victim die from a gunshot wound, Florence?"

There was a pause of several seconds, and Fuseli didn't need to see an anxious face to understand the robot was hesitating. Finally it said, "That is correct, Dr. Fuseli."

"Who shot him?"

"A member of our security personnel."

"I see. And *why* was he shot?"

"As his body altered, Mr. Grigoryan became violent. It's a common reaction among the victims, I'm afraid."

"All of them have become violent?"

"Yes."

"And Mr. Grigoryan was threatening to harm someone?"

Again, a too long pause before Florence responded. The robot was well programmed, Fuseli thought. One might think Minister Abbas had programmed it himself. Or had Florence been programmed, even designed, by the eccentric Klaus Gaithersburg? Inventor of the Merger device?

At last Florence replied, "Mr. Grigoryan killed another one of our colonists, Dr. Fuseli. A valued member of the med team here, in fact, and my former colleague—a Dr. Zhen Sung."

"I see," said Fuseli. "Good to know this … finally."

"Mr. Grigoryan attacked me, as well, but of course inflicted no real damage. It was after he had already killed Dr. Sung—and after having attacked me for trying to intercede—that security arrived and was forced to shoot him. Rather like the circumstances there on the Lancet, Doctor."

"Yes, rather like that … rather a lot like that. So how exactly did Grigoryan kill Dr. Sung?"

This time, with the cat out of the bag, the robot answered immediately. "Mr. Grigoryan drove the ends of his right arm's ulna and radius bones through Dr. Sung's eyes, and into her brain."

Part Four

Port Haven

A rotating wheel space station, Port Haven consisted of two great rings, each radiating eight docking arms. The Lancet slowed to match its speed to the station, and carefully nosed in to one of these arms, where at last it was locked in place. This longest leg of the journey was over. From here it was only a short jump by shuttle to Hydra.

Pluto and its largest moon Charon circled each other around the barycenter between them, their respective faces tidally locked in a timeless staring contest. Hydra orbited the Pluto/Charon barycenter at a distance of over forty thousand miles, whereas Port Haven simply orbited Pluto itself, closer than any of its moons. On Pluto and on Charon, both, were extensive military bases ... not to mention the military craft always ready to launch from Port Haven itself. These fortifications formed the outermost defenses for Earth's solar system.

Here at Port Haven, a portion of the E.C.S. Lancet's medical staff would rotate out to be replaced by fresh crew members. The Lancet also replenished Port Haven's medical supplies, and upon departure would be transporting a number of special patients back to Earth, to receive care that even this little city in space couldn't provide. The Lancet would be docked for a number of days, so even those crew members who wouldn't be cycling out would have time to disembark from the ship for a change of scene. However, Fuseli and his companions would be grabbing their shuttle to Hydra in only three hours.

Fuseli said a quick goodbye to those he had interacted with most on the Lancet, particularly thanking the hospital ship's captain and Security Chief Val Okoro. Then, he himself disembarked alone from the Lancet and headed for the office of General Aaron Stroud. Along the way he was greeted by citizens who recognized him from time he had spent living on Port Haven in the past, and military personnel always stopped to give a sharp salute. Even those people who disliked the often controversial medical officer still generally respected him, and some were even afraid of him.

There was always at least one Colonial Forces soldier on guard outside the door to Stroud's office; two in times of conflict of one kind or another. This soldier saluted Fuseli and buzzed him into the office, and immediately Fuseli stopped in his tracks and his face crinkled in an atypical grin. He had expected to see one friendly face in this room, not two.

"Captain," said Lieutenant Morris Tarragon, giving a respectful salute despite their long familiarity. Tarragon was a human wall, tall and broad, the Black man's scarred face normally quite intimidating, but at the moment he wore a big, sincere smile himself.

From behind his desk, General Stroud said, "I thought you might like a trusted man to watch your back on Hydra, Bob. I hear this guy isn't too bad at what he does."

"He's all right, I guess," Fuseli said, crossing to Tarragon and giving the man a hug, clapping him on the back. "I thought you were in Punktown, Morris," he said.

"Yeah," Tarragon said. "There were some terrorist threats directed toward the Earth Colonies offices, but it didn't turn out to be anything too big or well organized. My team made some arrests, turned the small fry over to the locals to deal with."

"Glad to have you with me again," Fuseli said. If there was a Colonial Forces officer Fuseli trusted even more than Aaron Stroud, it was Morris Tarragon.

"You healed up good now?" Tarragon asked. "How's Rhan?"

"Good, and good."

"Me, I started seeing a Choom lady," Tarragon said. The Choom were the indigenous race of Oasis, the exoplanet on which the fast-growing colony city called Paxton, but nicknamed Punktown, had been established.

Fuseli raised his eyebrows. He refrained from asking his friend what it was like kissing a Choom. Though almost indistinguishable from Earth humans in all other ways, the Choom had wide mouths that spread back almost to their ears. In any case, he was just glad his friend was seeing someone new, after his recent divorce. His ex-wife and their son currently lived in a Martian colony city. She'd grown tired of her husband being away for such extended periods; a common drawback in their line of work.

"Really?" Fuseli said. "Well, I'm sorry you got pulled away from her on my account. So what's her name?"

Stroud cleared his throat. "I know I orchestrated this little reunion, but maybe you two can save the small talk for the shuttle ride to Hydra? Which, if I may remind you, takes off in less than three hours."

"Sorry, sir," Fuseli said. He took a seat opposite Stroud, while Tarragon opted to remain standing, straight as a stone column.

"So," Stroud said, "what's your impression of Congressman Abbas?"

"Frankly? He's very pleasant. Too pleasant. Fake as any politician. I sure don't appreciate that he keeps me in the dark like he does."

"The Hydrans are very protective of their community, Bob."

"So you've said, sir. Permission to speak freely?"

"I thought we already were, with that last question."

"General ... of course, as per the oath of my profession, I want to do whatever I can to help stop these deaths on Hydra. But if I had my way, that would mean removing those goddamn Merger things from the back of their skulls. Clearly it isn't safe for them to be using this technology."

"They've been doing it for seven years now," Stroud countered, playing devil's advocate, "and they haven't had these problems until recently."

"That we *know* of. Look, what concerns me most is that they bolt these things into the heads of *children*, too. Everyone who's a part of that colony ... *every*one!"

"Hey, look, I'm not comfortable with that aspect, either. If it were just the adults, making adult choices, then—"

"It's a cult," Fuseli cut him off.

"Now, Bob," Stroud said sternly, pointing a finger at him, "I forbid you from using that term on Hydra. Or to any Hydran, even in confidence."

"I hear you, sir," Fuseli said. "However … still speaking freely, as you permitted me … it just seems weird to me that they've even been given a whole moon of this solar system to themselves, for this … *community* of theirs."

"A whole moon?" Stroud chuckled. "It's Hydra, Bob. That ugly little rock isn't even thirty-two miles at its longest point. Who else would want it?"

"It's still within close reach of the military bases on Pluto and Charon. So they have their privacy, but protection nearby if they need it. Not to mention their quick access to civilization in the form of Port Haven. Sounds like nice real estate to me."

"Nice real estate. Listen to you, Bob. It's just an empty icy rock."

"No more so than most of the moons in this system, only … yeah, smaller and less pretty." Fuseli leaned forward in his chair. "Colony Hydra is sanctioned by the Earth Colonies, but in the end it's its own independent entity. No wonder people are suspicious of them … while they paint themselves as being these poor victims of prejudice. How did they pull that off, sir? Does it just come down to money?"

"Of course it does," Stroud said. "That's no real secret."

"Okay, right, but the question is *why?* Who would support the creation of a good-sized colony on a pea-sized moon, and why?"

"For one, look no further than Abbas himself," Stroud said. "He was born into money. How do you think he got to be a congressman? But more significantly, it has to do with the empire of the late Klaus Gaithersburg. Gaithersburg, Incorporated. Old Klaus with all his various business ventures made enough money to ball up into a moon bigger than Charon."

"Who took over this empire of his after he passed?"

"Colony Hydra itself," Stroud said. "That is, its governing body."

"Which Rusul Abbas is the head of."

"Indeed. While Klaus was alive, Abbas was his righthand man."

"So they don't do any mining on Hydra, or any other type of industry? But then they don't need to, do they? They can just sit back and let the money pour in from all Gaithersburg's operations, which are spread from Earth to Oasis."

"True enough. As I say, with the company headquarters being Colony Hydra." Stroud smiled, trying to make a joke of it. "Look at it this way, Bob … you should be proud that the people who run such a powerful company agreed with my suggestion to bring you in to help. And this, even after they looked into your record and saw what a mean bastard you can be."

Fuseli heard Tarragon give a little snort, but the Colonial Forces lieutenant's face was stony when Fuseli gave him a look.

"I want to know more about the whole thing with the Merge, as they call it," Fuseli stated. "They can be as private as they want with the outside world, but they're bringing me in to help and I need to know all I can learn if I'm to do that."

"Then earn their trust, Bob. Be patient, be empathetic and receptive … not confrontational."

"Do you even remember who you're talking to, sir?"

"I mean it."

"And I mean it, too, General," Fuseli said. "I want to understand what this alien race they call the Nought is all about. I don't care how much money they have … how can they keep their knowledge of an alien race, and their relationship to it, all to themselves? It's unheard of."

"It's … a highly unusual situation."

"I will find out more about the Nought, from an outsider's perspective," Fuseli vowed, "if I have to undergo the Merge myself."

Part Five

Hydra

-1-

As the shuttle approached Hydra, Fuseli sat up front with the pilots rather than in the passengers cabin with Abbas and Tarragon and the others. To get a better sense of the place where he'd be staying for the unforeseeable future, he wanted to have a good look at the moon through the little ship's front window, in addition to the various views of it the cockpit's viewscreens provided. He had seen Hydra before, of course, when leaving the solar system on various missions, but never up close. Let alone landing on it.

"Got to be the ugliest moon in the solar system, sir," said the pilot as the body in question grew before them. "Looks like a potato. A deformed potato."

"Looks like a giant rotten molar, to me," Fuseli grumbled. The brightness of the moon's coating of water ice added to the effect. "Pulled out by its roots."

The copilot added, rather poetically, "A tooth from a dead god."

It was Fuseli's understanding that Hydra's unusual shape was the result of two bodies having collided in Pluto's orbit countless ages ago, fusing into one misshapen mass. Letting his imagination run with that image, he found it appropriate ... given how the Hydrans claimed to merge themselves on a regular basis with an alien race on a world so distant it was said to lie far beyond the reach of even the most remote of the Earth Colonies network's jump Chutes. These Chutes were massive constructions—interspersed through explored space—that served as artificial wormholes, and it was only by way of these wormholes that interstellar ships could reach a far-flung exoplanet like Oasis. At least, until interplanetary teleportation was achieved, though Fuseli's last mission, on Titania, had proved that research attempts were far from safe at this time.

Though the moon was unusual in shape, and tiny at less than thirty-two miles in length and nineteen miles in width at its shortest point, once the shuttle got close enough to Hydra it started to look like any other desolate moon of ice-covered rock. At this point, by simply looking out the spacecraft's forward window, Fuseli might have thought he was returning to Titania. God forbid.

But now, unique features started to come into focus below in the form of Colony Hydra, and the pilot contacted the base to let them know they would be touching down shortly. Instructions came back for which landing pad was available to them.

"Thanks for bringing the Minister back to us," said the voice over the com brightly. "We've missed him."

"Happy to oblige," the pilot responded.

Fuseli craned his neck, watching from behind and between the two pilots as the colony grew larger and spread wider before him. Colony Hydra had showed continued expansion over the past seven years, as more and more colonists migrated to settle there. The buildings, of various shapes and sizes, all radiated out from one large central structure … asymmetrically, depending on what the surrounding terrain allowed. Among the varied structures Fuseli noted a good number of large, linked geodesic domes, used for the growing of hydroponic crops. The domes' stress-supporting lattice patterns put him in mind of the hexagonal markings he'd seen on the skull of Josef Elmi.

One of the outermost of the colony's numerous connected buildings was still under construction, and there appeared to be a number of trucks or similar vehicles clustered there, manned by human crews, until Fuseli saw they were actually large robots extending slow-moving but powerful mechanical arms. Such machines had likely preceded any colonists when this settlement was first begun, except for a skeleton crew of human engineers.

The feature that commanded Fuseli's attention most, however, was naturally the enormous deep space satellite dish at the settlement's center. For a base, it stood atop the roof of the colony's long, low central building, the dish supported in a web of scaffolding and tilted toward the mysteries that lay beyond this solar system. It was impressive, at two hundred and fifty feet in diameter, though Fuseli knew there were much larger satellite dishes to be found throughout the Earth Colonies. But … *those* satellite dishes weren't linked to technology developed by that enigmatic genius, Klaus Gaithersburg.

Though its movements were imperceptible from up here, Fuseli knew the satellite dish would be in constant motion to keep its face pointed in the desired direction, compensating as Hydra tumbled wildly in its rapid and erratic rotation.

"Is everything made from green materials here?" Fuseli asked, because it certainly appeared that way. From the buildings, however diverse, to the satellite dish and its skeletal support framework itself: all the same shade of green as the Merger devices, not to mention that robot they had dubbed Florence. Fuseli didn't doubt that up close, these surfaces would hold the same oil slick iridescence.

"We call it the Emerald City," said the pilot, who had obviously shuttled people and supplies to and from Colony Hydra on prior occasions. "I don't know if the color is natural to the materials they use or only cosmetic."

"The color of money," Fuseli said.

"Coming in now," the copilot announced. "Deploying landing gear." He punched a few keys, and then added in that same poetic tone, "Welcome to Hydra—the many-headed dragon."

"We'll see about that," Fuseli murmured.

-2-

As the shuttle was rotated on its landing pad platform, to be aligned with the telescoping umbilicus that would be extended to it, Fuseli went back into the passenger cabin to grab his gear. Watching Abbas, Izzy, and the four security personnel in their black uniforms do the same, he bent his head close to Tarragon's and remarked in a low voice, "Not to be too paranoid, but we'll watch what we discuss in private from here on. We don't know if and when we'll be observed and recorded. When we're alone, we'll use the scrambler."

He tapped his wrist comp. It wasn't a common feature on such devices, but the military-grade device he and Tarragon wore could emit a scrambling signal that was able to disrupt the audio and even video of a wide range of hidden surveillance cameras.

"Got ya," Tarragon said, and both men straightened and picked up their duffel bags. They began to file out of the small craft after the others, to enter into the umbilicus. As they shuffled along, Tarragon nodded toward the security people. Several of them repeatedly cast looks back at the two Colonial Forces officers, just as wary as they. "Don't these people ever take their helmets off? They just trying to look tough?"

"I think I know what it is," Fuseli said. "If they're residents of Colony Hydra, they have Mergers stuck to their skulls, too."

"Then they're Colonial Forcers in name only," Tarragon grumbled.

"Well, maybe I'd consider them C-Forcers second, and Hydrans first."

"And maybe you should have been given more of a security detail than just me."

"Maybe. And maybe more of a med team than just what they have waiting for me inside. But if worst comes to worst, I'll just call General Stroud and tell him what I need here. We're only a hop, skip, and a jump away from Port Haven."

The two men—both wearing uniforms patterned in gray and black urban camouflage, with black greatcoats over that and the black beret that marked them as Special Ops—finally stepped into the collapsible umbilicus after the others. Outside this narrow tube lay the harsh environment of Hydra, minus 418 degrees Fahrenheit. Fortunately warm air blew through the tunnel, providing a breathable atmosphere, and the settlement's artificial gravity extended even here.

Only when the colony's head minister, Rusul Abbas, and his party had exited the umbilicus and passed into the concourse of the settlement's little spaceport did the four security guards finally remove their helmets, hold them under one arm, and turn to face Fuseli and Tarragon. As Fuseli had guessed, all four had a Merger fixed to the back of their head. Two were human men, one was a human woman with a head as hairless as Tarragon's and an expression almost as dour. The fourth was not human, and Abbas gestured to this being, smiling.

"You may have some stories to share, Captain," he said, "with our colony's chief of security, Murgan Larck."

For a moment Fuseli was silent as he took in the security chief. You didn't see many Gurm on the worlds or outposts of the Earth Colonies.

Yes, this individual—built on the scale of Morris Tarragon—was a so-called Green Gurm, which identified him as one of those the Earth Colonies had supported decades ago during the harrowing Gurm Conflict. It was the Yellow Gurm that had been the enemy then, but to be honest Fuseli hadn't seen much difference between the two brutal tribes, besides their differently-colored scales. Whether turquoise green or sunshine yellow, the Gurm were reptilian humanoids, not the fastest when it came to moving but frighteningly powerful if they got their clawed hands on you. Murgan Larck's face had a lizard-like snout, if more blunt, his golden eyes set in the front of his face like those of a human but still with nictitating membranes.

Larck's lipless mouth drew back in a smile, and the translating device he wore around his throat, obscured beneath a hanging dewlap, allowed his speech to come out as English ... though it still sounded raspy and mechanical. The Gurm were not the most technologically advanced of races.

"I'm sure we could compare notes," Larck said. "I too fought in the Gurm Conflict, Captain Fuseli. I piloted a Screamer class gunship. I may even have offered your platoon air support. But I was already a sergeant then, so I suspect I'm quite older than you. I understand you joined at eighteen years of age?"

"Yes," Fuseli said, indulging him. "I served three years as a field medic."

"My people appreciate your service."

"It was a, ah ... learning experience for me," Fuseli said.

"I also heard that in addition to being a dedicated trauma surgeon, who treated comrade and enemy alike, you were a fierce soldier with quite a body count."

"I didn't keep count," Fuseli said.

The Gurm's translator rasped a burst of static. Fuseli took this for a chuckle. "Very good, Captain. Ah, but that was long ago. We're so much older now, you and I, eh?"

"I told you you'd have a lot to talk about," said Abbas, cutting in. "But right now, I imagine you'd like to get settled into your dorm rooms, gentlemen. It's been a long, eventful trip here from Earth. Tomorrow, I'll see that you have a proper tour ... especially, of course, of our medical unit. Meanwhile, we'll be sure to have Josef Elmi's body transferred there."

"I'll also be wanting to have a look at the control center for your Merger system," Fuseli said. "I'm sure there is such a place."

Abbas's broad smile faltered subtly. "Yes ... yes, there is. But one thing at a time. Since I have many matters to attend to, that have built up in my absence, I'll have Izzy here conduct tomorrow's tour."

Fuseli turned to nod at the young woman, who once again wore her smart five-piece business suit, its skirt never having heard the concept of wrinkles. She smiled back at Fuseli and returned his nod.

"In fact," Izzy said, "I'll show you to your rooms right now."

"Sounds good."

"Until tomorrow morning, then, gentlemen," said Abbas as he turned away. Still holding their helmets, with their Drang assault engines hanging by straps across their armored chests, the four security guards started away with him. Seen from behind, it was all the more obvious that even Murgan Larck wore a Merger on the back of his hairless, scaly head. The Gurm cast a parting look back at Fuseli, his nictitating membranes blinking once mysteriously.

"Huh," was all Morris Tarragon had to say.

"Gentlemen?" Izzy said, sweeping her arm in a different direction. "We'll take a tram to the guest rooms."

"Lead on, lady," said Fuseli.

As they walked to the small, open-topped vehicle that waited for them, Fuseli glanced toward large vidscreens that ran both lengths of the spaceport, giving a view of the outside in lieu of windows for the purpose of greater safety. Along one side of the building he saw the row of landing pads, and on the other side—looming above the smaller structures that surrounded it—that colossal satellite dish, cupping its ear to the stars.

-3-

The tram was driven by a human being, rather than being autopiloted. Even here, there was ever a conscious effort to ensure that human beings were provided employment and not replaced utterly by machines. Except, Fuseli thought, in the case of the head of the med unit.

Sitting just behind the driver—who smiled like a mannequin and of course sported a Merger device on the back of his head—Fuseli asked Izzy, "Okay, so why the Emerald City thing?"

"The green color, you mean?"

"It is a bit conspicuous." After all, the floor, walls, and ceiling of the corridor the open little vehicle presently drove through were all of the same shiny green material. Even the tram itself. The driver gave a polite honk to warn a small group of strolling pedestrians of their approach. As the tram passed, one of the walkers waved. "It looks like some kind of enamel coating."

"You're probably aware that Klaus Gaithersburg primarily made his fortune through nanotechnology," Izzy explained. "He was a real innovator.

The trademark green color of all these surfaces you see, including our Mergers, is to indicate that Gaithersburg nanoparticles are embedded in the material. Even in the structure of these buildings themselves." She waved her arm at the corridor as they passed through it.

"What do these nanoparticles do?"

"They allow for programmable matter, for any number of reasons. Plus, they can communicate with each other—convey and receive information. Even our satellite dish is largely built from lightweight but durable nanomaterial, a hundred times stronger than steel."

"Huh. So why hasn't Gaithersburg's smart material become more widely used?"

Izzy smiled. "It will be. His legacy lives on, but it's up to us to help the public see him more as the genius he was, as opposed to the eccentric he's been made out to be by his detractors … mainly, competitors with ties to the media, not to mention the politicians whose campaigns they donate to."

"Gaithersburg had his own political ties; just look at Congressman Abbas. I hardly think he'd have been allowed to set roots down on his own private moon, otherwise."

"Well … the game has to be played, Bob."

They had left the spaceport and driven through tunnel-like connecting passageways into and through several other buildings, until they arrived at one of the structures that served to house the colonists. The tram slowed to a stop outside a row of doors behind which Izzy said were rooms reserved for guests to Colony Hydra.

"Do you get many guests?" Fuseli asked, as he and Tarragon retrieved their duffel bags and stepped down from the tram.

"Not many that stay long," Izzy admitted, also disembarking. "Mostly we see shuttles and cargo ships that just deliver supplies, or transport our colonists to and from work assignments abroad. Sometimes, due to a medical emergency or some condition we can't address here, a med team will come to transport a colonist to Port Haven."

"And none of these visitors are ever permitted to share recordings of what they see here, I take it?"

Izzy narrowed her eyes slightly. "Vids of most of the colony aren't a problem with us, Bob. It's just vids of the Merge, mostly, that are prohibited. That, and the technology that supports the Merge. And of course, anything that would be of a proprietary nature. We've had a few attempts at industrial espionage, which were luckily thwarted. The individuals were apprehended and our security force turned them over to the proper authorities to be dealt with."

"I see."

Again, playing tour guide, Izzy made a sweeping motion with her arm. "These first two rooms are for you and Lieutenant Tarragon. Take your pick. I'll transmit the pass codes from my wrist comp to yours, so you can have access to unlock and lock the doors as you wish."

Tarragon shrugged, ever deferential to his superior officer, so Fuseli said, "I'll take 700, on the end here. Morris can have 698."

"Sounds good." As Izzy was punching in some commands on her wrist comp, the housing of which was again of that shiny green material, a woman came walking down the hallway toward them and Fuseli looked up at her.

He saw that the woman was a Choom, a member of the race native to the exoplanet Oasis—reached only by interstellar ships making use of an Alcubierre drive system and artificial wormholes. She was slinky, with long legs bared by pajama shorts that matched her top, which was open halfway down her chest. She was even barefoot. Her face framed by long, straight, green-dyed hair, she gave Fuseli a smile that seemed twice as sultry for the extra width of her Choom mouth. She was carrying a bottle of wine.

The woman stopped in front of the door labeled 696 and buzzed. While she waited for an answer she glanced again toward Fuseli and Tarragon, smiling at both of them in turn.

Fuseli ignored the beep from his wrist comp that indicated Izzy had granted him access to his dorm room, instead watching the Choom woman as a voice came over the wall speaker for room 696.

"Hello," came a singsong voice, drawing out the word. "Who *is* it?"

The Choom woman leaned into the speaker. "It's Fhuum, baby—who do you think?" She held up the wine, for the door panel's security lens to see.

"All set, gentlemen," Izzy said, but Fuseli still ignored her as the door to 696 slid open and a man appeared in the threshold. He was gangly, with a curly shock of dark hair and a bushy mustache, barefoot also and wearing only boxer shorts and a white undershirt. The woman named Fhuum fell into his arms, giggling, and the man looked ready to kiss her until he noticed, with a jolt, Fuseli staring at him. The man slipped out of the Choom's arms, grinning embarrassingly.

"Oh, hi … are you Captain Fuseli?"

"That's me. And this is my security officer, Lieutenant Morris Tarragon."

"Great—hi, guys! I'm Marco Zarate. I arrived here over a week ago. Just had to jump over from Port Haven, you know."

"I know. Nice to meet you, Mr. Zarate." Fuseli stepped forward for a handshake. All the while, the Choom woman clung to Zarate's waist with one arm, still holding the bottle of wine in her other hand and never losing that lascivious grin.

"Well," said Zarate, "it's, ah, after hours here on Hydra, but I hope we can get together tomorrow and compare notes."

"We must," Fuseli said.

"Until tomorrow, then. Good night, guys!"

Zarate slipped back into his dorm room, along with Fhuum, and Fuseli might have thought the woman had come here to Hydra with him if it hadn't been for the Merger device that capped the back of her skull. The door to room 696 slid shut.

Fuseli put a hand on Tarragon's arm and said, "Sorry you had to find out your new girlfriend is cheating on you, Morris."

"That's hilarious, Captain," Tarragon said stonily.

Izzy was smiling. "Yes, it seems Mr. Zarate wasted no time in making friends here."

"I hope he doesn't get too distracted from his mission."

"Oh? But didn't *you* meet someone during your last mission, Bob?"

"Point taken." Fuseli tapped a key on his wrist comp, and the door to room 700 slid open. "Success."

"Very good," said Izzy. "Then, I guess I'll be saying goodnight to you two gents. If you need me for anything at all, please just buzz me. And should you get the late night munchies, if you continue right down to the end of this dorm hall you'll find a little cafeteria with all kinds of food machines."

"Very good. Then goodnight, Izzy."

She started away, but paused to look back and say, "Just let me know when you're fully rested, and I'll get started on a proper tour of the colony … and introduce you to our med unit."

Fuseli gave her a wave, then he and Tarragon faced each other meaningfully.

"How convenient," Tarragon muttered, "that a Hydran beauty has become so chummy with our special diagnostic tech, so quickly."

Fuseli put a finger to his lips, to remind his longtime security chief of the need for discretion. "Could be innocent."

"Could be he's already compromised," Tarragon whispered, before turning toward the door of the room alongside Fuseli's own.

-4-

The walls, floor, and ceiling of Fuseli's guest room were again of that green alloy embedded with nanoparticles, and he was almost surprised that the sheets and blanket of the bed weren't green, as well. He had just stepped out of the room's shower stall and dressed in his camo pants and a black t-shirt when his wrist comp buzzed. He slipped it on and answered, expecting to see Izzy Higgins on its screen, but it was the scaly face of Security Chief Murgan Larck.

"Captain … Lieutenant," the Gurm said, having included Tarragon in the call. "We have an incident in Dorm 6A … that's the residence hall at the end of your own, if you take a right. Room 603 … can you meet us there?"

"I'm on my way," Fuseli said, grabbing his holstered gun off the little bedside table and clipping it to his belt. Barefoot, he burst out into the hallway to see Tarragon had already emerged. Together, they started jogging down the hallway in the direction of the cafeteria Izzy had mentioned the night before.

The cafeteria turned out to be a nexus point, branching off in four directions, but they headed down a right hand hallway as Larck had indicated. People seated at some of the cafeteria tables, enjoying coffee and snacks before their work shifts, watched them pass with curious and concerned looks.

Down toward the end of this door-lined hallway, which at its entrance they'd seen labeled Dormitory 6A, the two Colonial Forces officers spotted Larck and four other security people. Only Larck was without his helmet. Another colonist, in civilian clothing, leaned against a wall clutching her arm and one of the security people was helping support her.

When Fuseli and Tarragon reached the group, Larck informed them in his translated voice, "We have another change … in there." He nodded at the door numbered 603.

For the moment, Fuseli instead turned his attention to the woman who clutched her arm, and he saw blood welling up between her fingers. She looked greatly distraught, besides being in pain from her wound. "How are you hurt?" he asked her.

Before the woman could answer, Larck said, "It's just lacerations … I've already called the med unit to get a tram down here to pick her up. She was lucky she got out of there quick. Lucky, too, that the person inside doesn't seem to remember how to get the door open."

Through gasping sobs, the injured woman reported, "Jonas is my coworker, at the Farm. He hasn't shown up for work in three days, and he wouldn't answer calls, so our boss sent me down here to look in on him."

"Your boss should have called *us* to do a welfare check," Larck cut in.

Fuseli ignored the Gurm's interruption. "What happened?"

"I buzzed, but he didn't answer the door. I saw it was unlocked so I let myself in. Then … then … he saw me. Oh my God … the sounds he was making." She wagged her head violently, as if to shake away the memory. "He came rushing at me … swung at me with those … arm things. He hit me, here." She nodded at her deeply gashed arm. "But I shoved him back and got out the door before before he could come at me again. I couldn't lock it, but like Murgan says … it's like he doesn't know how to open it."

"He must have done that Merge thing on his own, in there," Tarragon said.

"Yeah," said Fuseli. "Three days ago."

Larck gestured toward the black-uniformed soldier who was positioned closest to the door. "When we open it, she's going to hit him with a tranq dart. It might not work, owing to the changes to his body. If that doesn't take him down alive, we'll probably have to kill him. You okay with all this, Captain?"

"Sounds reasonable. I mean, it's not like we could change him back to the way he was before, is it?"

"Highly doubtful," Larck said.

"Just hang on … wait for this woman to be moved out," Fuseli said, watching as a tram turned the corner into the hallway. This tram was all white, with a red caduceus emblem. It came humming down the dorm hall toward them, and when it was near enough two med techs leaped out to attend to the wounded woman. They walked her to the little vehicle, where the driver slipped behind the controls and the other tech immediately saw to the bandaging of the farm worker's torn arm..

As the tram started away, Fuseli went to draw his pistol. Tarragon was doing the same, but Larck saw this and held up a clawed hand.

"Sirs. We allowed you to keep your sidearms here as a courtesy, but please leave matters like this to us. You're here in a medical capacity."

Fuseli removed his hand from his pistol's grip. "As you like, Sergeant."

Larck stared at him for several beats, his nictitating eyelids blinking twice, before he replied, "The Gurm Conflict is long over, Captain. I'm Security Chief now."

"Of course ... sorry, Chief."

Fuseli felt a tad guilty for purposely using the wrong title, as if to put the security man in his place. He just couldn't help himself sometimes.

"All right," Larck said, facing the door. "Remember, let's not bottleneck going in. Are you ready, Corporal Gerling?"

The female Colonial Forcer raised the front of her bulky, blocky-looking Drang assault engine. Its various muzzles could fire anything from blazing red energy beams, to automatic bursts of solid bullets, to mini rockets, to shotgun pellets ... plus tranquilizer darts. Though, such formidable military killing machines seldom made use of those.

"Ready, Chief," Gerling said over her helmet's mic.

"Let's do this," Larck said, and it was he who reached out and stabbed a finger into the key that opened room 603's door.

The green panel slid back, and from behind Larck's people Fuseli saw Corporal Gerling duck into the room. Larck himself was close on her heels.

A naked figure crouched low to the floor in the middle of the small, single-occupant dorm room, tucked almost into a ball, with arms tightly wrapped around its legs. At the sound of the door whisking open, its head lifted and turned toward the intruders with a speeded-up, jerky motion. From between the four flexing mandibles that had once been human jaws, a series of clicking sounds and wet popping noises were emitted, and the strange figure was already unfolding its limbs and rising to its feet.

That was when Gerling pointed her Drang at it and fired a single tranquilizer dart, which struck the creature in the throat.

Instantly, the thing that had once been a colonist named Jonas was gripped with convulsions, falling onto its back and flailing all four limbs, its feet pounding the floor. The strange sounds it made had grown louder and frenzied.

Larck waved for Gerling to keep back, as they waited to see how long it might take for the tranquilizer to take effect. Meanwhile, two more security people had entered the room and fanned out, but they hung back also. This allowed Fuseli to get close to the room's threshold, as the last member of Larck's team remained outside with Drang ready to cover the doorway in case the creature made a run for it. His Drang was doubtlessly not set to dart mode. Tarragon covered the door, too, his hand ready to go to his gun, Larck's wishes be damned.

Fuseli now more clearly saw the entity that lay flopping on the floor, as if it were being electrocuted. Given more days for the deformities to progress, this individual was more transfigured than any of the previous five victims … and yet, the changes to his body had not killed him. One might not even have believed this had once been a human being, had they not already been aware. Much of the man's original flesh and underlying tissue had sloughed off, and Fuseli saw wet clumps of it strewn around the room. Atop a desk, resting beside the man's wrist comp, was a folded-over flap of meat from which a single human eye, filmed white, seemed to stare. The room stank of bottled-up decomposition.

What was left of the man was nearly an animated skeleton, somehow held together with ligaments and tendons, and whatever pared-down muscles it had retained. The ribs and pelvis showed white through the barest translucent casing, and vertebrae had pushed out the back like a row of spines. And of course, halfway down their length the arms had split into two independently moving limbs, all four of which were tipped with a hook like a tiger's claw.

Fuseli saw a new development with this victim. His legs seemed jointed backwards, calling to mind the hind legs of a horse, and without shoes it could be seen that the feet had divided down the center, every other toe having dropped off and the remaining two replaced with hooks like those at the ends of the arm bones.

And then there was the head, which had shed anything soft that could be called a face. Even the tongue had dropped out, discarded near the foot of the bed. The raised hexagonal pattern that covered the enlarged, almost spherical skull was more distinct than ever, and the bone had even grown around the edge of the Merger device affixed to the back of the skull, as if to absorb it.

"Jesus," Fuseli heard one of the security people say over his mic, "how can he even still be *alive?*"

"Jonas!" Larck snapped at the thing, as it continued convulsing. So far the drug hadn't seemed to take effect, beyond these violent spasms ... and was it the tranquilizer causing that, or simply the creature's response to being attacked? "Can you hear me?" The Gurm pointed his own Drang at it, ready to give up on taking it alive.

"Try another dart!" Fuseli called.

Before Larck could make a decision about giving Gerling that order, with shocking suddenness the creature leaped to its feet, whipped around to face the woman who had darted it, and sprang toward her through the air with such force it seemed those newly configured legs were what enabled it to do so.

The thing crashed into Corporal Gerling and she was slammed backwards into one wall, the Drang knocked sideways in her hands. From the doorway, as he drew his Scythe handgun, Fuseli saw the transformed colonist clawing at Gerling in a blur of four hook-tipped limbs. Gerling could be heard crying out in helpless terror over her helmet's mic.

"Get off my soldier!" Larck roared, rushing in.

"Sir!" one of his team members cried, as he leveled his Drang. "Get out of the way, sir!"

Larck was heedless, as he got up close to the creature that still clawed wildly at Gerling. Together, the two had slid down the wall to the floor, with Gerling on her back and the creature straddling her.

And then, Larck pointed his Drang only a couple of inches from the thing's orb-like head and pulled one of his weapon's triggers. This was for the Drang's shotgun feature. One of the gun's multiple muzzles erupted with a brief flash, and with a silenced *poof* of discharge the skull of the man formerly known as Jonas, who had worked on the hydroponics farm, was shattered into flying shrapnel.

The creature folded onto Gerling, dead, and she kicked it off her in horror. The other two security people in the dorm room rushed forward then, and got her to her feet.

"Captain," Larck said, not looking around at Fuseli as he stood over the crumpled figure, his reptilian face almost achieving a human-like scowl, "please see to Corporal Gerling."

"Call back that medical tram," Fuseli said, as he removed Gerling's helmet, her arms helpless and dripping blood. "Let's get her—and that body—to your med unit."

-5-

Fuseli had boarded the little med tram along with the wounded Corporal Gerling, while the responding pair of med techs quickly got the twisted, transformed corpse into a body bag and loaded in the back. Without her helmet, Fuseli saw Gerling was that bald-headed Colonial Forcer who had been among Abbas's security detail. Her face, dour and intimidating when he'd seen her before, was now wrenched with anguish.

"He clawed my arms all to fuck, sir," she managed through clenched teeth. Her helmet and black chest armor had saved her from lethal injuries, but the sleeves of her black uniform top were shredded and soaked in blood. "Am I going to bleed out?"

"Not on my watch, soldier."

As the tram got underway, leaving the others—Tarragon included—to catch up later, Fuseli dug into the vehicle's supplies to tend to the woman himself. First off he placed a pressure bandage over a nasty laceration on the woman's neck. The creature had managed to land a strike under Gerling's helmet, but it had missed the carotid artery.

"What's your name, soldier?"

"Corporal Gerling, sir," she winced.

"*First* name."

"Eva, sir."

"We'll get you all patched up, Eva," Fuseli told her. "You'll be fine … but I see a little vacation to Port Haven in your future."

"Is that necessary, sir? I'd prefer not to leave here."

Fuseli met her eyes. "Why?"

"Well, this is my *home*, sir." Her eyes beseeched him. "This is where I *Merge*."

The med techs unloaded the body bag onto a collapsible stretcher and wheeled it into the med unit, while the robot the Hydrans called Florence stepped into the corridor to help Fuseli get Gerling onto a second stretcher.

"It's a pleasure to meet you in person, Dr. Fuseli," Florence said in its pleasant female voice. "Even under such unfortunate circumstances."

Fuseli saw that the robot again displayed the seemingly alive face of an Asian woman on its head's face screen, and he assumed this was its default look. At least it knew enough not to stammer with him anymore. Together, they wheeled Gerling into the med unit.

"Bay One, Doctor," Florence indicated, pointing.

"I want her under anesthesia immediately," Fuseli said. "Her arms are a mess. Looks like muscle and nerve damage. I'm going to work on her myself."

"As you wish, but I'll be happy to assist you."

"I want that corpse put on an examination table … I'll get to it when I'm done with her. But damn it, I wish Larck hadn't shot it in the head. I'd have wanted to examine that more closely, and I hope the Merger wasn't ruined. Should have shot it through the throat … he could've taken the head off clean."

"I'm sure Chief Larck did the best he could under strenuous

circumstances, Doctor."

"Well," Fuseli said, as he helped transfer Eva Gerling onto the surgical bay's operating table, "I can't honestly say that I blame him."

Gerling gazed up at Fuseli, her face gone pale and eyes child-like as fear and shock mixed into something like awe, watching as he unsealed and removed her body armor. Next he'd be cutting away her top. Meanwhile, Florence prepared to administer anesthesia.

"It's an honor to have you work on me, sir."

"Just like the good old days of the Gurm Conflict," he told her.

"Oh my God," said Marco Zarate, a hand cupped over his nose and mouth. "I've only seen the Mergers already removed from these things … never one of the bodies in person."

The corpse of the farmer named Jonas Mikkelsen lay face down on a table in one of the med unit's several examination rooms, what was left of its head mostly held together by its Merger device. Zarate and Fuseli watched as Florence lowered a mechanical arm from an array of such limbs clustered above the table. The robot explained, "This is the tool with which I can remove a Merger, when it needs to be replaced with another."

"So they're regularly known to malfunction and need replacement?" Fuseli asked.

"No, never … not before these six recent victims, Doctor. A Merger might need to be replaced, though, when the subject is a young child and they outgrow it."

"So just how young are children here when they first get implanted?"

"At six years old, Doctor. Not before then."

"Six fucking years old," Fuseli repeated.

The robot paused with its hand on the arm it had lowered from above. "You disapprove, Doctor?"

"Of course I disapprove … Dr. Florence."

"Technically I'm not a doctor, sir. I'm—"

"Never mind. Just pull that thing off so we can give it to Mr. Zarate." Fuseli faced the diagnostic technician. "This one's going to be different."

"How so?"

"There are six pins that secure these devices to the subject's head. They don't penetrate far into the bone … except in this case, that is. Before you got here, when we scanned this victim we saw the pins had elongated somehow … as if not only this man's body was changed, but the Merger device, too."

"How could that be?"

"How could any of this be? But from studying the units you've looked at so far, you'll know they're made from some patented Gaithersburg alloy. A smart material."

"Yes. With nanoparticles incorporated."

The two men turned back to watch the overhead arm, as with a soft whirring it withdrew the six pins that held the Merger in place. Prior to this, of course, Florence had used a delicate saw to remove the bone that had grown over the edges of the device. With the pins retracted, the Merger was detached and Florence took the unit into its mechanical hands. It held the device out, to show the six long protruding pins.

"Jeez!" said Zarate. "Those had to have gone right into the brain."

"Chief Larck didn't leave the brain intact for us, but they obviously did," said Fuseli.

"The Mergers don't need contact with the human brain to function," Florence said, placing the device into a nearby sterilizing unit so it could then be handed off to Zarate for study. The sterilizer came on with a violet glow inside. "Only proximity."

"Maybe this Merger wanted to function even better," Fuseli said.

"But was this Merger influencing his body or was his body influencing the Merger?" Zarate asked.

"They were merged. They did it together." Fuseli looked in the direction of the med unit's front office area, which also served as a waiting room. Zarate had arrived here with his Choom lady friend, Fhuum, but she waited for him out there playing a game on her wrist comp. He continued, "Nanoparticles are used in gene editing, so I thought maybe the nanoparticles embedded in the Mergers are migrating into the victims and wreaking havoc, but scans don't detect the presence of Gaithersburg nanoparticles in their bodies … just the usual types of nanoparticles any of us might have ingested as food preservatives and the like. And yet, I'm seeing that these people have had their genetic structure rewritten."

"Crazy!" said Zarate.

"What have you found out so far, about why or how these units are causing this phenomenon?"

"God, Captain Fuseli—nothing. Sorry, but I'd never even heard of tech like this before. The units from the first four victims don't seem any different from new units I've been shown that have never been implanted in anyone yet."

"Nevertheless, it has to be that some powerful influence is acting through the Mergers to bring about these massive changes, whether that influence is intentional or some kind of side effect of Merging."

"*Intentional?* Are you saying—"

"Florence," Fuseli said to the robot. "Every single part of this man is altered in some way … a little or a lot. The first few victims may have died from such alterations, but this one remained viable for three days, and may have continued to do so had he not been discovered."

"Indeed, Doctor … it's beyond perplexing."

"Look at this leg, for example. The metatarsal bones have lengthened into something like a horse's cannon bone. That's what I'm talking about. And look at the skull—or what's left of it. It no longer has eye sockets, or apparently any visual organs. Was that why it couldn't open the door? And yet it knew where Corporal Gerling was when it attacked her, so it seemed to be sensing her somehow. Maybe it has something to do with this patterning on the head." Fuseli tapped a shard that remained intact. "It's almost like one big compound eye, like an insect's, but made of bone.

Whatever's causing this is using the resources available to it."

"Truly fascinating," said Florence, nodding its head. The face on its screen nodded along with it.

"I'm going to ask you what I've asked others." Fuseli pointed at the corpse with its bizarre ruined skull. "Is this what the Nought look like? Is that what the Mergers are trying to recreate here, from human bodies?"

"*What?*" Zarate said, flicking his wide-eyed gaze from Fuseli to the corpse and back. "You mean … whoa! Maybe, like, as an army to invade us? Because they're too far away to reach us across space physically?"

"Doctor," said Florence with mechanical calm, "as others have no doubt told you, no one knows what the Nought look like. Even Head Minister Abbas would have no idea."

"So he says."

"But I assure you of it, Doctor."

"You haven't Merged, have you? So you only know what you've been told."

"I can't experience the Merge, you are correct. Only organic beings can do so. Perhaps if I had an encephalon computer." Florence tapped the side of its head with one finger. The robot referred to a type of bioengineered artificial brain grown from organic tissue, which was utilized in certain robots and computer systems.

"But when a human Merges, don't they experience the sensations of the Nought they're linked to? Wouldn't they have an awareness of the alien's body through its own perception?"

"It doesn't quite work like that, but you really must speak further with Minister Abbas or someone else who can explain the experience. Again, as you say, I only know what I've been told."

The sterilizer pinged. Florence removed the Merger from inside and reached for a receptacle to place it in for Zarate's study, in the tech lab he had been assigned for his needs. Watching this, Fuseli complained, "Guess I can ask them again what they experience. All they can do is not tell me much of anything … as usual."

-6-

Lieutenant Morris Tarragon sat on the edge of his dorm room's bed, watching as Fuseli sat at the room's little desk and spoke with General Stroud, at Port Haven, on his wrist comp. Tarragon's own wrist comp was emitting that scrambler signal to hopefully disrupt any surveillance equipment that might be eavesdropping.

Fuseli had just finished filling Stroud in on the day's events. "Jesus, Bob," he said. "And you've suggested to Abbas that he should tell all the colonists to refrain from the Merge until this phenomenon is understood, and safeguarded against?"

"Of course I have, sir. Early on."

"Strongly suggest it again. How can this Merge experience be so important to them that they'd put their lives at risk? That they'd risk this horrible mutation thing happening to their *children?*"

"All I can think is that this experience they rhapsodize about has become an addiction with them. That's why doing it as a community isn't enough for them, so they even do it alone in private. What I want to do is perform a brain scan on one of them while they're undergoing the Merge, to see how it effects the brain."

"It's like a major dopamine hit, huh?"

"Maybe something that basic. Or maybe something we've never seen the human brain experience before. Something it *shouldn't* experience."

"But they won't let you witness the Merge," Stroud stated.

"Correct."

"Push Abbas on that, Bob. Push him … but tactfully."

"I'll keep at it."

Stroud sighed. "Were you able to save that injured woman's arms?"

"Yes, sir. She'll have proper use of them both, but she'll be laid up here for a bit. She expressed that she'd rather not be shipped over to Port Haven. The first woman this colonist wounded is fine—already back to work."

"Thank God. I wonder why these victims, when they change, always become so violent."

"Good question, sir. Good question indeed."

For convenience, the tech lab that had been set up for Marco Zarate wasn't far from the med unit in the colony's maze-like complex of buildings, and when Fuseli and Tarragon walked there on foot and let themselves inside, it was to find Zarate leaning back against a work counter with Fhuum kneeling on the floor in front of him. At the sound of the door sliding open, Zarate let out a gasp. Fhuum only looked around at the men casually before taking her time standing up, her long-lipped Choom mouth smirking.

Zarate fumbled his raised organ into his trousers and managed to get his fly closed. "Sorry … oh my God, sorry you saw that."

"Should have locked the door, baby," Fhuum sighed.

Fuseli asked her coldly, "Don't you have a job to report to?"

"Yeah, I'm a manicurist, but business is slow most days."

"A *manicurist?*" Tarragon said.

"Yeah, at my mother's salon. She has a whole chain of salons on Oasis, too. Not everyone in our colony lives a life of drudgery like they do on other colonies, my man. Some people here have no job at all."

"Well, *baby* here has a job to do," Fuseli said, "so you can go now."

"I'll be nice and quiet."

"I *said*, you can go now, and you aren't to come into this lab again. You can see Mr. Zarate on his time off."

The Choom woman looked Fuseli up and down and snorted. "You can't boss me around … I'm not in the military."

"Time to leave," Tarragon said, taking a step toward her. "Or you'll see what we can or can't do."

"Please, hon," Zarate said nervously, knowing better than she what Special Ops officers were capable of. "I'll see you later, you know that."

"Okay, okay, assholes," Fhuum said, backing off toward the door. "But if you think you can bully me while you're here, I'll complain to Minister Abbas himself. He'd kick you off Hydra sooner than he would me."

With that, the Choom woman departed, and Tarragon crossed to the door and locked it himself.

Fuseli blasted Zarate with the black lasers of his eyes. "You need to remember why you're here, Mr. Zarate, and act like a professional. I mean it … she is not to step foot in here again—ever."

Zarate gave a tremulous little chuckle. "You make it sound like she's a spy or something."

Fuseli glanced at Tarragon, who tapped his wrist comp to indicate that he'd activated the scrambler and it was likely safe to talk. Then, Fuseli got up close to Zarate and leaned in. "Of course she's a spy," he said. "Not to be cruel, Zarate, but do you think she's fallen in love with your amazing good looks?"

More than Zarate's organ was deflating. "Well, she said … you know … that I'm kind of cute … "

"Anyway," Fuseli cut him off. "Anything about this new Merger?"

"I only just got it a little while ago, Captain, you know that … but … " He turned and gestured toward the unit, which lay on a lighted scanner bed atop one of the room's equipment-laden workbenches. "The thing was hit by a piece of buckshot … you can see the dent in it. I think because of that, probably, it isn't functioning anymore at all. And as for the securing pins, it looks like they were designed extra long in this one unit, but that doesn't seem likely, does it?"

"I wouldn't think so. Not long enough to penetrate the brain."

"Well, changing shape *is* a property of some smart materials, so … "

"All right, look," Fuseli said, cutting him off again, "I have a side project for you." Onto an uncluttered corner of workbench he set down his duffel bag, which he'd carried here with him. As Zarate watched, Fuseli lifted out a large black orb. It was Corporal Eva Gerling's helmet.

"This is the helmet of the Colonial Forcer that Jonas guy attacked. It has a body cam, here." He tapped a finger against the front rim of the neck area. "I can see that it recorded the incident."

"And? You want me to play it back for you?"

"I know how to play it back if I put the helmet on, but I can't send a copy of the recording to my wrist comp. There's a security wall in place to prevent that. What I want you to do, then, is play the recording here and try to translate the sounds Jonas was making."

"Captain, I'm not a linguist."

"But you can presumably run a translation analysis, *right?* The sounds could very well be nothing, but see what you come up with. Can you manage to keep your second brain in your pants long enough to do that much?"

"Yes, Captain," said Zarate, throwing a jumpy look at Tarragon, looming by the door. "I'll do my best."

They left Zarate to his projects, and as they stepped out into the corridor Fuseli asked his friend, "Is your girl anything like that?"

"Not quite," said Tarragon. "So what's next?"

"I do believe Izzy still owes us the grand tour."

-7-

"I'm sorry Minister Abbas can't join us himself," said his aide, Isobel Higgins, "but he's still bogged down in work that piled up while he was on Earth. He's aware of the latest incident, though, and believe me it disturbed him greatly. He truly appreciates that you tended to Eva yourself, Bob."

Tarragon sat up front in the emerald-colored tram beside the driver, who was another Colonial Forcer outfitted in the colony's solid black security uniform, but at least he was without a helmet, revealing the Merger capping the rear of his head. Fuseli and Izzy sat beside each other, in back.

To start out, they were on their way to the linked series of sizable geodesic domes in which were grown a variety of organic foodstuffs to feed the citizens of Colony Hydra. They called this the Farm, as Fuseli had already been made aware. Naturally, other sources suppled the colonists' nutritional needs as well, including vats of fermented bacteria that could be shaped and flavored in any number of ways—from mock pasta to mock meat patties—and living insects and fish, not to mention certain prepackaged commercial items that were occasionally shipped in on cargo vessels, to stock snack machines.

Fuseli said, "I get the impression that now that we're here to do our thing, your head minister is avoiding us."

"Not at all, Bob. As I say—"

Fuseli interrupted, "After what happened to Jonas Mikkelsen, has Minister Abbas had second thoughts about allowing all you colonists to continue with the Merge, while our investigation is still ongoing?"

Izzy smiled at him wearily, wagging her head. "Bob … I don't know what more I can say about that, that I haven't already said."

"God damn it, Izzy," Fuseli hissed, losing patience. "I think there's a whole lot more you can say about that … if you'd only educate me on how the Merge works, and what it's actually like."

"Again, Bob—"

"No," he snapped, "I mean it. Is our tour today going to include the auditorium or temple or whatever the hell you call the place where you gather for your community Merges?"

"The Ceremony Chamber," Izzy said, her tone having grown a trifle chilly. "And no, I'm sorry … we won't be visiting there. Anyway, at this time there'll already be a shift of colonists inside, participating in the Merge."

Fuseli swore under his breath, but reined himself in. "At least tell me where the Ceremony Chamber is, for the sake of curiosity."

She sighed. "It's below the satellite dish."

"Oh? I would have thought the control center for the dish would have been there, and the mechanism that keeps it oriented toward the Nought."

"You're right about that. The Ceremony Chamber is the next level down, beneath the control center. It's a subterranean level. Or should I say, a sub*Hydran* level."

As they neared the Farm, the tram came upon a large, circular chamber with an open front facing onto the corridor. A park had been established inside, right down to a floor of synthetic grass and a sprinkling of potted plants and trees. The roof of the park chamber was itself a geodesic dome, and through its lattice Fuseli could see Pluto. Owing to the dwarf planet's small size, and the great distance of Hydra's orbit from it, Pluto wasn't all that large in the black, star-bejeweled firmament. Nevertheless, Fuseli could still make out the bright, heart-shaped region on its surface called Tombaugh Regio.

The tram slowed to a crawl, so Izzy could show off the park. There were swing sets and other pieces of playground equipment, and currently about a dozen children clambered on and around them noisily, watched over by two teachers, presumably, sitting on a bench. One of the adults noticed the tram and waved pleasantly, and Izzy waved back.

Fuseli couldn't help but notice, of course, that the oldest four or so children already had smaller versions of the Merger fixed to their skulls.

Tarragon twisted around in his seat, and the look he and Fuseli shared didn't need to be verbally expressed.

"Are any Gaithersburg products manufactured on site?" Fuseli asked, as the tram picked up speed again toward the domes of the Farm.

"No," said Izzy, "there are manufacturing centers on Earth, Mars, Oasis, elsewhere … but you could say our most important research and development labs are here on Hydra."

"So you're saying the Merger units aren't manufactured here?"

Izzy hesitated before answering. "I didn't say that. The Mergers *are* produced here."

"Where?"

"In a building we simply call the Plant. It's underground, too. Close to the Ceremony Chamber."

"Okay, and you're not going to let me see that, either, correct?"

"We … we don't know yet."

"Are you telling me you haven't even let Zarate see it yet? It could be crucial in helping him understand what's going wrong with your tech!"

"It *may* be allowed, Bob ... we're waiting to see! Waiting to see if you and Mr. Zarate can figure out the problem by examining the bodies of the victims and their Mergers!"

"Do you think I'm some kind of industrial spy? I don't know how you people expect us to work this way, Izzy. You're tying our hands!"

"This is it, just ahead," she said, thrusting out her chin to point. Her jaw was tight, her voice gone fully cold. "The Farm."

"Great ... a salad would really make me feel better right now," Fuseli said, but then he recalled General Stroud's orders about conducting himself with civility here, and so he bit back whatever other venom he might have spilled. For now, at least.

But Izzy lowered her forehead into one hand, eyes closed, and said, "You're right ... I know you're right. At the very least, we should have already let Mr. Zarate see inside the Plant."

Encouraged, Fuseli laid his hand on her arm and spoke in a gentler tone, remembering his bedside manner. "You must, Izzy. Please ... you *must*. Enough is enough. We're here to help you people, not hurt you. It's time to trust us."

The tour included the satellite dish control center, which was mostly automated, but not the subterranean level below it. Still, Fuseli glanced around nonchalantly for the means by which to descend, and saw several unlabeled doors in the control center that might possibly lead to stairs or an elevator.

After a stop at a surprisingly pleasant little restaurant for lunch, Izzy directed them to the Hydran Colonial Office. This was where Head Minister Abbas conducted his business—both for the colony and often for the Colonial Congress as well—along with his cabinet of twelve lesser ministers.

As Izzy led Fuseli and Tarragon through the outer offices so as to meet these other ministers, two security guards fell in with their party. Fuseli didn't take it personally. While they walked—Izzy exchanging greetings with various people in office cubicles along the way—Fuseli asked her, "Are these ministers also on the board of directors of Gaithersburg, Incorporated?"

"Yes," she said, "as a matter of fact they are. They're pretty much one and the same."

"They must be very capable individuals, to be running a good-sized colony *and* such a powerful company."

"Well yes, they are impressive individuals … just like Minister Abbas himself." Before reaching the conference room where the ministers would be waiting to meet with the Colonial Forces officers, Izzy stopped and spoke with Fuseli in a hushed tone. The pair of security guards kept a polite distance. "Bob … please don't bring up the matter of requesting access to the Plant just yet, all right? Let me talk to the Head Minister about that in private first. I promise to do my best."

"So what *are* we going to discuss in there now?"

"You can share your findings on the investigation thus far, though the cabinet is always kept up to date on everything anyway. Mostly the other ministers just wanted to have the opportunity to meet you in person, and thank you for coming to Hydra to help our people."

Fuseli sighed. "Okay, I'll be good. But do me a favor … talk to Abbas *soon*. I want me and Zarate to have a look at the Plant."

"All right, all right."

"And while you're at it, tell him I want to see the Ceremony Chamber, too."

"Bob … "

"*And*, I want to witness a Merge."

"Come on, that part just isn't possible. Maybe … *maybe* he'll let you see the Ceremony Chamber between Merges, but no one is allowed to witness a Merge who isn't Merging. *No one*. Please, *please* don't push things too far."

Once more Fuseli had to rein himself in, and it took a considerable effort, but he said, "Look, just do what you can, but the sooner the better—for the sake of your people." He waved his arm before them. "Lead on. For now I'll content myself with a little handshaking if I must."

"Thank you, Bob, thank you. The more reasonable you are, the more likely they are to honor your requests … within reason."

"But just between us … in the end, I'm not here to kiss asses, no matter how powerful Gaithersburg, Incorporated is. I'm here on Earth Colonies business."

"But don't forget, Bob, "Izzy replied. "Head Minister Abbas is an Earth Colonies congressman. There comes a point where *he* doesn't kiss asses, either."

-8-

Only minutes after leaving the conference room, and shaking thirteen hands—including, not for the first time, that of Head Minister Abbas—Fuseli was already forgetting the ministers' names and faces. He'd met plenty of colonial functionaries in his day, and these people didn't strike him as any different, despite their double duties. All of them, even the women, in five-piece suits that only varied in shades of gray, all quick with toothy smiles that convinced him less than those affected by Florence's Asian avatar.

"Izzy mentioned you have some requests," Abbas had said to Fuseli as he guided him out of the conference room, patting him on the back as they went. "I promise that you and I will talk very soon."

Fuseli had grunted his thanks. He hoped soon meant soon.

Before they left the Hydran Colonial Office to move on to the last stop on their tour—the colony's power plant, which housed its reactor—Fuseli excused himself to use one of the outer offices' restrooms. "Two coffees at lunch," he explained to Izzy with a straight face.

“Take your time, then,” she said.

Fuseli asked Tarragon, “Do you have to go, too, before we hit the road? No? Are you sure? I won’t ask again.”

Tarragon didn’t dignify his commanding officer with a reply.

Fuseli found he was the only person in the men’s room, aside from one man whose shoes he saw under the bottom edge of a toilet stall’s door. He made use of a urinal, went to the sinks, bent and splashed cold water in his face. It was hard work, this reining himself in when lives were on the line … and the people who had summoned him for help were the same people who willfully obstructed him.

He lingered there at the row of sinks for a few moments, eyes closed, listening to the almost subliminal hum of the hidden processes that kept everyone in these fragile little buildings alive in an environment hostile toward life of any kind. The circulation of air and heat and power, not to mention the process that supplied Earth-like artificial gravity.

Just as he was opening his eyes and preparing to head for the exit to rejoin the others, he heard another sound from behind him.

It was a brief string of clicking noises, followed by several odd, wet pops. Then … quiet again, apart from the perpetual thrum of the colony’s vital processes, and the muffled voices of office workers beyond the exit.

Fuseli turned slowly, and saw that directly behind him was that stall with the shoes showing under its closed door. *Christ*, he thought, even the walls of the toilet stalls here were emerald green.

“Hello?” he said aloud. “You okay in there, buddy?”

No reply was offered.

Moving warily, Fuseli crossed the distance to the stall door. “Hey in there—you all right?”

Again, no answer. No sound of movement of any kind, not even that of a bowel movement.

Fuseli hesitated, then rapped his knuckles on the door. “Look … I think you’d better—”

As if the rapping had shocked awake the person in the stall, they immediately sprang up from the toilet and flung open the door so hard it banged into the inner wall.

The appearance of the figure standing inside the stall didn't surprise Fuseli. The man's white office shirt was saturated with blood and his face had slid off his skull, as if he had been flayed alive but his torturer had lost interest before cutting it away from his neck, where it hung inside out. The creature thrust its eyeless face at Fuseli, opened wide its four mandibles, and uttered a louder, more rumbling string of clicks. But the creature didn't pose for Fuseli to examine these details for longer than the tick of a second, before it was plunging at him with its four hooked forelimbs extended from the colonist's blood-soaked sleeves.

Fuseli had been ready for this, though, and he sidestepped the creature, which was carried forward with its momentum. It nearly crashed into the sinks before catching itself and whirling, furious, to rasp another series of clicking sounds at Fuseli. By now, he had pulled his handgun and pointed it at the transfigured colonist's chest.

"Stop," he said. "I don't want to hurt you … I really don't."

The creature advanced on him more slowly, cautiously than before. One menacing step … another. Its split, hooked feet cramped into those shiny dress shoes.

"Try to understand what I'm saying," Fuseli said to it. "You're a *man*. A man who works in this office out here. Do you have a family on Hydra? Are they waiting for you to come home from work?"

Another step. A few inhuman popping noises from deep in the throat. Those forked arms spread wide, the riven jaws twitching.

"You're still a man in there," Fuseli repeated, backing off a step. "Why do you want to hurt me?"

It wasn't so much compassion that prevented Fuseli from simply killing this man, though of course he was not lacking in compassion. But he knew the man was too far gone, and what kept him from shooting was scientific curiosity. Chiefly, wanting to gauge whether there truly was anything left of the man's identity, memories, and reason. Or had those all become hopelessly warped, as well?

The thing suddenly stopped advancing, and cocked the many-faceted, bony globe of its head as if it were struggling to decipher an alien language.

Then, the restroom's door opened and another of the office workers entered, whistling brightly.

"Fuck," Fuseli hissed.

Startled, the creature spun toward the whistling sound, as if it pierced its newly configured skull, and leaped at its former coworker. Fuseli swung his handgun around to follow it, but the office worker—his whistling abruptly cut off and eyes gone wide with alarm—was in the line of fire.

Just as the creature had almost reached the man with its outthrust arms, and Fuseli was about to make the split-second decision to risk a shot, the restroom door opened again and there stood Lieutenant Morris Tarragon, his own Scythe in his fist. With his free hand he shoved the office worker out of the way, and then he blasted the thing in the chest with a double tap. The force of the nearly point-blank impacts blew a pair of yawning pits out the creature's back, which sprayed fragments of spine like scattered dice. The thing flew back, hit the floor, and flopped two or three times before going still.

As the office worker fled from the restroom, in a panic but fortunately unscathed, Fuseli went to stand over the corpse, and Tarragon said to him, "I decided I had to use the restroom, after all."

"He must have been sitting there on the toilet Merging," said Fuseli. Now he had been joined by others in the restroom, including Head Minister Rusul Abbas himself, all standing around the grotesque corpse in its puddle of blood. "You people really are addicted, aren't you? Is that how you keep recruiting new members and growing your numbers here? One taste of bliss and you're hooked?" He was done reining himself in.

Abbas looked up from the body at him. Fuseli hadn't noticed before how the man's bearded cheeks had become haggard, that dark bags were forming under his eyes. He appeared too weary to bite back at Fuseli's rebuke. Instead, he said, "Captain ... I give you and Mr. Zarate permission to see the Plant. Also, the Ceremony Chamber ... between Merges."

Fuseli blew out a long breath, then said, "Thank you, Minister."

-9-

They stopped by the lab provided to Marco Zarate, to pick him up immediately before Abbas could change his mind about having a look at the Plant. Fuseli and Tarragon were driven to the lab in the same tram, by the same driver, in which they had been touring the colony before the violent incident. Abbas, Izzy, and perhaps others would meet them at the Plant. Abbas first wanted to let his other cabinet members know about his decision. This made two deaths now among Abbas's administrative staff—the office worker, whose name Fuseli had learned was Bryce Corrigan, and Izzy's fellow aide Josef Elmi—and maybe that was too close to home for him.

When Fuseli entered Zarate's lab, he half expected Fhuum to be there and he was prepared to tear into the diagnostic tech, but Zarate was alone ... and grew excited when Fuseli told him where they were headed.

"How's that translation coming?" Fuseli whispered to him as they climbed into the waiting tram.

"Still running it," Zarate said. "Not sure that crazy noise is going to amount to anything more than growling or whatever. So far no luck, but then again these translation programs have never heard anything like it before."

The tram took them back toward the settlement's central structure, upon which the great satellite dish was perched, always turning its face outwards ... toward wherever it was in the cosmos the Nought were said to dwell, whether that be a planet or a space station. Maybe, Fuseli thought, they were a band of outsiders or misfits themselves, with their own colony on some godforsaken moon.

Fuseli, Tarragon, and Zarate met the others in the dish control center. The other party consisted of Abbas and two lesser ministers Fuseli had met a few hours earlier, and Izzy, plus Security Chief Murgan Larck and two other security members armed with assault engines.

"As you can see," Abbas said, "my fellow ministers agreed that allowing you to have a look at the Plant could prove helpful, in some way we hadn't thought of."

It's about time, Fuseli wanted to say, but he only nodded.

"But please," Abbas went on, "I must insist … no vids are to be taken." He nodded at Fuseli's wrist comp.

"If you insist."

Together, they all crossed the room toward one of the unmarked doors Fuseli had noticed earlier that day, set back between long counters full of control panels and monitor screens. Presently the only two occupants of the large control room were a male human tech and a robot identical to Florence, except that the avatar on its head screen portrayed a young Black man. The robot nodded to the party of humans, the avatar smiling handsomely.

"Fucking blackface," Tarragon muttered.

Windows spaced around the large room gave a view of the sprawling colony buildings, radiating out from this one, and beyond that the rumpled icy landscape of Hydra. Again, Pluto stood out vividly against the inkiness of space, and off to its right was its comparatively large moon Charon. This view made Fuseli reflect on the notion that there were children in this colony who had been born here, and had never known any other sky, or landscape, than this one. Still, before he allowed that thought to depress or anger him, he reminded himself of the hellish major cities of Earth.

Abbas used his wrist comp to unlock the door he'd led them to, and it slid back to reveal a lift cabin as surprisingly roomy as that of a freight elevator. As the group filed in, Fuseli asked the congressman, "Is this the only way down?"

"It's the way we're using," was all that Abbas would say.

Once all were inside, Larck—who was nearest to the controls—hit a key and the elevator door closed. As the cabin began to smoothly descend, Fuseli again addressed Abbas.

"You once told me there's a control center for the Mergers. I'm going to guess that's part of the Plant, or adjacent to it."

"They're basically the same thing," Abbas admitted. He still looked uncomfortable making these concessions, as if he resented the inevitability of it. "The Plant is where the Mergers are manufactured, and where all Mergers are linked to the master system."

"Makes sense," Fuseli said, "that it would be below the dish."

"Precisely."

"Please, Minister Abbas, I really need to know more about the Merge right now. About the Nought. Not just this sketch I've been given."

Abbas held up a finger, as if to advise a student to maintain patience. The elevator had stopped descending and its door whispered open. "We're here," he said, and they all began to disembark.

The Plant, which Fuseli now knew also encompassed the Merger Control Center, spread before them, mostly presenting itself as an open-plan work area. At least, this first room, which was quite large but with a low ceiling, *feeling* subterranean, though there looked to be other rooms and corridors that branched off from it. The thrum Fuseli had been conscious of in the men's room earlier was stronger here. He supposed the workers, technicians, and researchers he saw distributed throughout this open workspace had become accustomed to it, but for him it felt like someone strumming the strings of his nervous system. It was an unpleasant sensation.

Near the elevator was a large upright floor screen, such as one might see at Port Haven advertising a new movie or product, that immediately caught Fuseli's attention. He stopped to take in the vid it was playing in a loop. It portrayed workers in the process of constructing a new, good-sized space vessel. Wherever that was, there was atmosphere: no need for protective suits and helmets. In the distance loomed a city skyline of immense buildings.

"What's this?" Fuseli asked, motioning toward the screen.

Tarragon stepped forward and said, "I know that place—it's Phosnoor Shipyard, in Punktown."

"Paxton," Abbas corrected, preferring that city's proper name. Pride entered his voice, displacing some of the gloom that had come over him. Presenting the achievements of the company he'd essentially inherited was something he was more comfortable with. "Indeed it is. What you see here is Gaithersburg, Incorporated's first starcraft ... which when completed, hopefully in only two or three months more, will be christened the E.C.S. Merger."

Fuseli reached out to expand the screen's image with movements of his hands. No, he hadn't imagined it: the interstellar ship under construction appeared to be entirely emerald green in color, with its signature iridescent sheen. "That special alloy of yours can even withstand space travel?"

"It's ... related to the material the Mergers are made from," Abbas said.

"Looks like a cargo ship," Tarragon noted. "Or a construction ship. What are you going to be shipping ... or building?"

The pride Abbas conveyed increased, and he actually grinned. "We'll be shipping materials to build more jump Chutes. And then, yes, we'll be building them, too."

"*Chutes?*" Fuseli said. "Your company is going to make its own jump Chutes?"

"Yes, but naturally they won't only be for our use ... which is why we've been given the go-ahead to construct them. They'll be accessible to any world or colony within the Earth Colonies network. You see, currently the remotest Chute is far, far short of where we've ascertained the Nought to be. That is, within our ability to determine, at this stage of the game. So, we ourselves will be building a series of artificial wormholes over the upcoming years, to get us closer and closer to them." He raised a hand as if to ward off any objections before they actually came. "I know ... the Nought are thought to be so distant from us that it could take decades of this process of building and passing through new wormholes to actually reach their world. But, that's not the primary objective anyway. Our more realistic goal is simply to place satellite dishes on other worlds, farther and farther out with each jump. The result, of course, being that the connection we make with the Nought will become ever stronger and stronger."

"Whoa," said Zarate, looking a little glassy-eyed. "What an ambitious project. You people are amazing."

"Are your new Chutes going to be made of that same fancy alloy?" Fuseli asked, pointing at the screen.

"That's correct."

"Insane," Tarragon murmured, just loud enough for Fuseli to hear.

"Of course," Abbas continued, "our approach will be different if the experiments on Titania with interplanetary teleportation come to fruition. Then we could shave many years off our project, by leaping instantly from planet to planet instead of crawling there on starcraft, that would have to be manned largely by robots."

"This Chute project is all news to me," Fuseli said. "Well, I mean, of course I've known new Chutes were planned, but I didn't know Gaithersburg had the contract."

"Well, you know by now we like to keep a low profile. But also, this entire endeavor has only recently been approved. I admit, though, we were already constructing this ship before those approvals came in. It was a gamble, but thank goodness in the end we got the thumb's up. In time we could have a *fleet* of these construction ships."

"Besides the robot crews, there will be human pioneers who'll be willing to go," Izzy said, her blue eyes almost luminous. "Who'll be *excited* to go, even if they end up spending decades of their life—or even the *rest* of their life—on that journey. Just think of the sights they'll see, that no one has seen before! Honestly, I'm considering signing up myself!"

Abbas put a hand on her shoulder warmly. "I'd hate to lose you, Izzy, but you know I'd never stand in your way."

"I knew Gaithersburg, Inc. had money," Fuseli said, wagging his head as he continued watching that screen, "but not this much."

"Beyond our company profits, which are considerable," Abbas said, "we also have many generous—and powerful—sponsors and investors. Not to mention the vital support of various politicians, and scientific branches within the Earth Colonies government."

"I'm thinking not all the heads of the hydra are talking with each other," Fuseli mused aloud.

"Captain?"

Fuseli tore his attention from the vidscreen, and nodded toward the open-plan area they were about to venture into. "So what about all this?"

-10-

Adriana Bezerra's husband hadn't wanted her to move the twins to Colony Hydra, and in fact he was still challenging her guardianship of their children in court, but Minister Abbas himself had promised he'd do anything to protect the three of them … and was even paying for her legal fees himself, so she had little fear that Noberto would succeed. Still, it hurt her that he was denouncing her to anyone who would listen, even threatening to have her charged with child abuse for allowing the twins to be implanted with Mergers. As if fourteen-year-olds were helpless little infants! If only he would speak to his children about it, they would surely tell their father in gushing terms—as they told their mother—how wonderful they felt the Merge was! However, Adriana wouldn't allow her ex-husband to contact any of them.

Yes, of course, when the three of them had first come here, almost two years ago, and the twins had realized they needed to undress to join the group Merge in the Ceremony Chamber they'd been reluctant … Gabriela in particular. She was very self-conscious about her body, which was then filling out its adult contours prematurely. Now, however, they couldn't wait for their daily shift. So eager were they to Merge that they did so here in their apartment every day, additionally … sometimes several times a day.

Making herself a cup of tea in their little dorm room apartment, Adriana was at that very moment thinking of Rusul Abbas. In fact, missing him, for he had been away for a while on Earth for business reasons, and now since coming back he'd been preoccupied with work that had accumulated in his absence—let alone this matter with the mysterious deaths of her fellow colonists. Since his return she'd only spoken with Rusul twice in calls, not in person, and then any further calls to him had gone unanswered. Sometimes, when she had a few glasses of wine in the evening, she entertained the idea of marching herself down to the Hydran Colonial Office and buzzing at his door, or better yet the door to his own apartment, but of course either idea was out of the question. Those two places were guarded by a pair of soldiers around the clock, even when Rusul wasn't within, and from the start of their involvement he'd impressed upon her the need to be discreet.

"Filho da puta," she muttered to herself, cursing him in Portuguese, as she stood at the kitchen counter staring through the steam coming off her cup of tea. Also from the start, she had known she wasn't his only woman here at Colony Hydra … and she didn't doubt he had other lovers on Earth. He was divorced himself, after all, and she couldn't claim him any more than anyone else, but that didn't stop her from hating the other women he saw in the colony. The ones that she *knew* of.

If only they were part of the same shift in the Ceremony Chamber, but they weren't … despite her efforts to change hers. At least then she could *see* him, even if it would still be unwise for them to be seen speaking to each other intimately. He had to keep up a respectable appearance, after all, if he was to strengthen the reputation of Colony Hydra—and his reputation in the Colonial Congress. Ah, but maybe it was actually for the best that they were on different shifts. She'd hate to see him nude in the Ceremony Chamber, where every other woman, man, and child could see him just as easily as herself … rather than nude just for her, in her bed when he sneaked here in the middle of the night.

Thinking of Rusul undressing for the Merge in the Ceremony Chamber made Adriana remember that it was nearly time for the shift she shared with Gabriel and Gabriela. They'd have to get moving if they didn't want to arrive late. There was a point at which the doors were locked, and no straggler would be admitted.

She glanced at the time on her wrist comp … an expensive model of iridescent green alloy, that Rusul had gifted to her. One or two more minutes to sip her tea before she shepherded them on their way.

The kids were very quiet behind the closed door to the room they shared. It was only a two-bedroom flat, and the last time Rusul had been here—lying in bed beside her, as they engaged in some post-coital pillow talk—she'd asked him if it was possible that he could have them moved into a three-bedroom apartment instead. After all, the twins were getting older now and really shouldn't be sharing a queen-sized bed as they did.

"How about two single beds?" Rusul had said, smiling as he traced a finger around one of her nipples where it poked up through her long, blonde-dyed hair. "Twin beds for the twins."

"Rusul, come on, they shouldn't have to sleep in the same *room!*"

Rusul had chuckled then, tweaked her nipple teasingly, and said, "I'll tell Izzy to look into that for you, okay?"

But now, here it was all this time later and still no word about a move to a larger dorm room. Maybe little redheaded Izzy was denying her on purpose, since Adriana had her suspicions about Rusul sleeping with *her*, too. That freckle-faced, big-eared bitch.

She hadn't wanted to tell Rusul that her concern about the twins sharing a bedroom was that once, when they were twelve, she had come in on them unexpectedly to find them … she wanted to call it *experimenting*. Plus, on two later occasions over the years she'd found them acting embarrassed and suspicious under the covers. She hadn't made a big fuss about it on those occasions, even that first time, because kids would be kids, and to some extent she felt it was natural that they'd be curious. Still, she didn't want it to progress any further, into something that might persist into adulthood ... especially when there were so few potential mates here at Colony Hydra. Well, on that front, she could only hope that more and more people would settle here over the coming years, just as Rusul and his cabinet always promised all of them.

Adriana sighed, wondered why she had waited so close to her Merge shift to make this cup of tea, but she supposed she could reheat it later. She tilted up her head a bit and called out, "Kids! It's time to go! Get out here!"

She went to sit at the table in their kitchenette to slip into her shoes, and as she did so called out again, "Gabriela! Gabriel! Let's not be late to the Merge!"

She had to admit to herself, she was afraid to go into their bedroom unannounced these days, for what she might find going on—they were teens now, and hormones had to be popping—but they were running just too close. Adriana got up from the table, strode to their closed door panel, and rapped on it loudly.

"Kids! Move your butts!"

That was warning enough. She reached to the door control panel and punched the key to open it. At least they knew better than to lock their door when they were in there ... no way she would stand for that.

She had wondered if she might find them lying on their backs on top of their covers, without clothes but without doing anything untoward—simply in the middle of their own dual Merge. They even held hands whenever they did that, and she found it cute. After all, she had even joined them at times, naked herself. Merging wasn't something dirty ... it wasn't about giving in to the body's appetites, but *transcending* them. But would they really be indulging in a home Merge so close to the time of their group shift?

She saw they weren't lying atop the bed, however, or cuddling under the covers. In fact, she didn't see them in their shared room at all, though surely they hadn't sneaked out of the apartment. Or had they? She had napped a while ago, after an afternoon indulgence of a single glass of wine, so maybe they'd slipped out then, to see friends? Was that why she hadn't heard a peep behind their door for the past few hours?

"Guys?" she called out, stepping over the threshold into their room. She spotted an article of clothing flopped onto the carpet by the side of their bed, and snicked her tongue impatiently, going over to pick it up so as to drop it into their laundry hamper. As she bent to retrieve it, from the corner of her eye she noticed other articles of clothing scattered about the room … and just as she reached to pinch an end of the garment discarded by the bed, she finally noticed overlapping trails of dark, wet drops winding about the room, that she hadn't previously spotted against the carpet's green color … especially since the only light in the room came through the door she'd just opened.

As soon as her fingers touched the garment by the side of the bed she withdrew her hand with a little gasp. Wet … slippery. *Not clothing.*

Up close like this, even in the room's dimness, Adriana saw that what she had mistaken for an article of clothing was actually a good-sized section of human tissue, even with a patch of long black hair rooted into one end of it.

Adriana flinched back and let out a scream, and the sound of this caused two figures that had been crouched low to the floor on the other side of the bed to shoot up into view. Two bizarrely deformed heads, devoid of flesh and covered in strange honeycomb-like patterns, swiveled in her direction.

"Oh no, no, no!" Adriana cried out, spinning toward the door. Only a few steps and she'd be out of the room again, and she could hit the key to close the door, and she would then lock it herself …

She didn't make it even those few steps.

Together the reconfigured twins—stripped both of clothing and skin, but even now bearing a close resemblance to each other—scrambled up on top of the bed and launched themselves off its bouncy surface, leaping through the air and coming down on their mother's back. Well, they had always done everything together anyway, hadn't they? Under their weight they drove her face-first into the carpet, and already both of them were furiously slashing at her with their new forelimbs. Eight forelimbs all together, ending in eight eagle-like talons. They tore into the back of Adriana's neck, jerking out hunks of flesh that flew throughout the room to splat near the gobs of their own discarded tissue. They tore into her scalp, ripping her hair and the flesh it was rooted in from the glistening red ball beneath.

Adriana tried to appeal to them for only a moment, tried to get out one of their names. Would it have been Gabriela? Gabriel? All that came out was the first syllable, before the rest of it turned to a throat-ripping scream, which soon enough turned into only the gurgling of blood in her throat.

And still the twins kept tearing, flinging meat across the bed, against the walls, even sticking it to the room's glossy green ceiling. And all the while, from between their mandibles came streams of rising and falling clicking noises, punctuated by strange popping utterances, all of which conveyed the twins' combined rage.

-11-

Running down the center of the Plant's open-plan main room was the heart of the Merger manufacturing process. This long, rectangular area was completely boxed in with clear walls, extending right to the low ceiling, and the two dozen workers within those walls wore baggy white coveralls over their work uniforms, and white hoods over their heads. At both ends of the aquarium-like enclosure, in case there was a fire and one of the exits was obstructed, something like an airlock separated this cleanroom environment from what lay outside. These twin antechambers were gowning areas, in which workers donned or removed their outerwear.

In addition, whenever someone changed before entering or leaving the cleanroom they would be bathed in a violet-hued, sterilizing light.

Abbas invited his tour group to draw close to the cleanroom's walls so he could point out the various processes used in creating the Mergers, but as Fuseli stepped forward Security Chief Larck prodded his arm. A little wary, Fuseli paused and turned to him.

"Thank you for caring for my soldier, Captain," Larck said in his translated voice. "I visited her a short time ago. She's doing well."

Corporal Eva Gerling had been moved into her dorm room, where she would continue recovering from surgery.

"Glad I could help her," Fuseli said.

That was all; Larck was obviously not the chatty or emotional type. He simply nodded curtly, then he and his two security people hung back while Fuseli joined the tour group at the enclosure's wall.

Some of those within the cleanroom sat at workbenches, while others were required to move about more in the course of their duties. Among the humans were two robots, again of the same basic model as Florence, one with the face of a young Choom man and the other with the kindly face of a gray-haired woman.

"Hold on," Zarate said, bringing his nose right up close to the transparent wall. "This looks like injecting molding, here. Do the Mergers start as metal foam?"

"Indeed," said one of the two lesser ministers who'd tagged along, standing beside him. Fuseli struggled to remember the man's name. Moussa ... something Moussa. This minister—also on the board of directors of Gaithersburg, Incorporated—had adopted the same proud tone of Abbas. "As do all our buildings." He waved his hand around the room. "It's a quick process, and easier than transporting tons and tons of metal sheets to Hydra for construction. Outside, we inject the foam into frameworks built from scaffolding materials, just to sketch in the outlines. Then, a catalyzing agent is sprayed over the foam to solidify it. Obviously, where there's no atmosphere it's not going to harden up in the air."

"And the nanoparticles are already present in the metal foam state?"

"Correct."

Further along, they saw the molds opening and various parts of the Mergers being extracted. For pieces that started out as lightweight metal foam, Fuseli was surprised that they already came out looking so glassy smooth once the catalyst had been introduced into the molds. The various pieces then went down the line, where workers fitted thin, flexible sheets of 3D printed circuitry to their inner surfaces. Ultimately, the circuitry was sealed inside and the various sections of the Mergers assembled, fitted together like the plates of a skull. They ended up looking like little green bowls, but with six bone pins extending from the curved interior.

"Those pins are always the same length, right?" Zarate asked the youngish Black minister named Moussa.

"Yes, of course. There's no room for variance there, unless the Merger is meant for a child. And speaking of which, we make smaller-sized Mergers for children, as you can see over there on the other side. Not to mention, the plates of each and every Merger can be adjusted to allow for an individual's head shape … "

Zarate interrupted him. "I mean, the bone pins can't be lengthened … extended?"

"No. Once the unit's completed, there can be no changes to its outer form … aside from the adjustments I just mentioned."

"*Should* be no changes to its outer form," Fuseli said. "Because we've seen it happen, to the pins in Mikkelsen's unit."

Moussa said nothing to that.

Zarate asked, "Is there a chance I could take some of these circuitry sheets with me, back to my lab for study?" He pointed at the stacks of 3D printed sheets, waiting to be shaped to the Merger interiors. "I mean, I've disassembled the units from the victims, but I mean just the sheets in their raw state, straight out of the template."

Moussa and Abbas exchanged a look, before Abbas spoke up to say, "We'll consider it."

"He really needs to," Fuseli pressed. "Just looking at this stuff from out here isn't all that helpful in itself."

"Perhaps, Mr. Zarate," Abbas allowed, "if one of our technicians is present with you in your lab while you examine the circuitry. And then, removes it once you've finished with it. Also … just so long as you don't record any images or vids of it."

Moussa nodded, and the other minister—a gray-haired woman Fuseli remembered only as Sonya, her face not too dissimilar from that of the robot worker—gave her nod of consent as well, as if a vote had been taken.

"Thanks," said Zarate.

Izzy was waving at a few of the workers in the cleanroom, their faces smiling through the clear fronts of their hoods. Fuseli saw this and leaned in beside her ear. Her autumn-hued hair smelled good. "Everybody loves Izzy," he remarked.

In turning to face him, smiling, her face was close to his. "Even you?"

"If I was a younger man, I'd be pretty smitten."

"Maybe you'll still become smitten anyway," she said, keeping her tone quiet and private. "Hey, maybe you could even join me on my travel to unknown solar systems, if I decide to sign up for that. You might even captain the ship."

"Huh," Fuseli said. "You know, once I might even have wanted to … when I was a younger man. Just so long as I didn't have to have one of these—" he reached around to lightly tap a finger against the Merger that capped the back of her skull "—in order to take the job."

Tarragon spoke up to ask, "So all the Mergers your people wear start out in this one room?"

"That's right," the gray-haired woman named Sonya said, taking her turn. "But as more people join us in our mission, and we become more accepted and expand our community beyond Hydra, we hope to see more Merger manufacturing sites throughout the whole of the Earth Colonies."

"*Mission*," Fuseli muttered to himself, upon hearing the woman use that word.

"And for now," Tarragon asked, "every Merger is implanted by just Florence alone?"

"Well," the woman said, sounding a bit somber now, "Dr. Sung used to do so, as well … before she was killed."

"Over there, against that back wall," Abbas said, gesturing, "is where finished devices are boxed up to be carted over to the medical center."

"What's going on over here?" Zarate asked, having pushed on ahead of the others toward the end of the cleanroom enclosure. "What are these small units?"

"Ah," said Abbas, joining him. The others dutifully trailed after. "Here we're working on a prototype unit, that would be much smaller, as you can see."

On the other side of the wall, a seated worker swiveled in her chair and held up one of the freshly molded prototype units for the tour group to view, holding it between finger and thumb like a coin. Its inner surface bore only a single bone pin.

"Whoa," said Zarate, "that's tiny."

"It would fit right in under your hair," said the female minister, slipping a finger through the hair at the back of Zarate's head and almost seductively rubbing its tip against the man's scalp. "You wouldn't even see it."

"Have these been tested on people yet?" Fuseli asked.

"We've just begun that," said Moussa, "with a few volunteers."

"How *do* you test finished products, in general?"

"There are a number of tests each unit has to go through before it's approved for use, to ensure proper integration with the master system, and every tenth unit is tested on a living subject. We're very serious about quality control, Captain Fuseli."

"Tested on people where … in the Ceremony Chamber?"

"Oh no, right here in the Plant." Moussa pointed off toward a corridor that branched from the main room. "Down that way we have testing rooms, where a subject's Merge can be monitored."

"Is anyone in there right now?" Fuseli asked. "Can I see?"

Moussa held Fuseli's gaze for a beat before he replied. "No one's testing right now."

"If they were, would you let me see them?"

Moussa glanced at Abbas, so Fuseli faced the congressman instead.

"We might arrange that, the next time we run a test," Abbas said.

"And what about the Ceremony Chamber? Can we see that next?"

"I'm afraid not," said Abbas, consulting the time on his wrist comp. "It will have to wait. There's a shift of people Merging in there right now."

"What is it about the Merge ceremony, exactly, that isn't fit for the eyes of the uninitiated?"

Abbas seemed to struggle to articulate an answer, and looked irritated at having to do so. "It's all just part of the … the sense of bonding we share, as Hydrans. The *connectedness*. For anyone who's not part of that bond to be present would seem … an intrusion. Disruptive."

"The Merge process is sacrosanct."

"Yes. But not in the religious sense."

"Isn't it, though—really?"

"It is *not*. As we've said, we don't worship a deity. What we commune with is the Nought. And the Nought isn't only the race we call the Nought … the Nought is the great nothingness with which that race communes."

"I'm still not getting it."

"I have an idea," Izzy said, laying a hand on Fuseli's arm and looking back and forth between him and Abbas eagerly. "What if we were to fit you with a Merger, Bob?"

"Yes … *yes*," Abbas said, his eyes lighting up, too. "That would be the best way for you to understand, Captain. The *only* way."

Fuseli couldn't stop himself from chuckling in disbelief. "Are you kidding me? There's no way I'd consent to that."

"Bob," Izzy persisted, "just consider *trying* it! You could have it removed at any time if you wanted. Any Hydran is free to have their Merger removed! It can be done very easily, with no harmful result."

"We just saw a harmful result of having a Merger implanted, back at your offices," Fuseli reminded her. "Sorry … guess I'll just have to stay ignorant."

"You may change your mind later," Izzy insisted.

The last stop on the tour of the Plant was the Merger Control Center, in a somewhat smaller room adjoining the manufacturing room. Fuseli judged this spot to be directly below the center of the satellite dish control room, which was in turn directly below the base of the dish. Based on what Izzy had told him, that meant the Ceremony Chamber was close by.

To him, this control center for the Mergers looked much like the server room at Port Haven, which he had seen inside, but then Port Haven was a much larger space station than Colony Hydra was a colony. The rows of servers, looking like the bookshelves of a library, gave off that deep thrum he had felt upon arriving at this level, and in here he thought he felt it as a vibration in his teeth. As in the dish control room, the only technicians monitoring the banks of screens along its walls were one human technician and one robot, wearing the avatar of an Asian man with an elderly face of friendly crinkles.

Zarate seemed impressed with the tall rows of servers, and he went to one of them. "Are these brainframes?" he asked.

"Why yes," said Moussa, joining him. "Each drawer houses an encephalon drive. Together they form a very powerful network."

"May I?"

Moussa nodded, and watched as Zarate reached to the first server and pulled out one of many horizontal, drawer-like drives on its gliders. Inside this thin glass frame, which was filled with a greenish fluid to nourish it, was a gray, convoluted mass of bioengineered tissue that to Fuseli resembled a human brain flattened out like dough under a rolling pin.

"I'd say this is a powerful system indeed!" Zarate enthused. "You people just never cease to amaze me. And so all the Mergers are connected up to this?"

"They are," said Abbas. "And these servers are in turn connected with the satellite dish above us, to form a one-of-a-kind communication system. It's what makes the Merge possible."

While they talked, Tarragon took Fuseli aside and confided, "I'm almost tempted to take an implant temporarily myself, Captain, just so I could give you an insider's report."

"Don't even think of it, Morris. Even for a short time, there's no telling what kind of damage it could do to you … maybe something we aren't able to detect now, that would manifest later. Anyway, Izzy says they can have these Mergers removed anytime they choose, but how many of these cultists actually do that? Not many, I'd be willing to bet—if any. Once they're hooked, they're hooked. Addicted."

"I said I'm *almost* tempted," Tarragon clarified. "*Almost.*"

-12-

Amjad Idrissi worked in the power plant that kept all of Colony Hydra running. He wasn't qualified to work in the reactor room itself, but in his spare time he was taking lessons on the net to earn his certification. For the past three years that he'd lived in this colony he'd had to be content with mostly just being a glorified maintenance man.

His brother Fadel was the one who had enticed him into joining the colony, boasting of the money he made working at the headquarters of Gaithersburg, Incorporated. And it was true that Fadel had done well for himself, since he *did* have his certification to work with the reactor. In fact, he'd been on the team of engineers that had installed the thing, over seven years ago. Fahed had known how Amjad was struggling to scrape by on Earth, struggling even to find a wife, and had promised his younger brother a whole new life on the tiny, crazily tumbling moon called Hydra. Gaithersburg, Incorporated would even pay Amjad's way from Earth to

Hydra, if he would only commit to joining the colony there. And of course, on the condition that he welcomed a Merger implant.

Well, Amjad was doing better here, he had to admit, but he harbored a degree of bitterness. His older brother claimed to be too busy with his job and personal life to help Amjad study for his reactor certification, though he knew studying anything via the net or, even worse, via books was not Amjad's strong point. And despite getting by more easily here than he had been on Earth, where were all the available Hydran beauties Fadel had described in selling him on the move? Easy for Fadel to say—he lived with his wife Basma, who was expecting their first child.

Amjad knew he was no movie star when it came to looks, but he wasn't expecting a movie star for a mate, either. Pickings were simply too slim. Still, Fadel was always reassuring him that more and more women would settle in the colony over time … but more and more men would be migrating here, too, so the ratio when it came to competition would likely stay the same.

On several occasions, when things had just built up in him too much, Amjad had coaxed a certain robot assistant they called Jimmy to join him in one of the duct-like maintenance chutes that branched off from the power plant. The default image on Jimmy's face screen was that of a pleasant, dark-haired man in his forties, but when they were alone in the cramped chute, surrounded by thick bundles of cables bracketed to the walls, Amjad would whisper to the robot to switch to another avatar. This face was that of a dark-haired female in her late teens, perhaps, with an appropriate voice to match, who might as well have been Jimmy's daughter. Then, because it had no useful orifices, Amjad would have the robot service him with one metal hand. This had always got the job done, but not in the most satisfactory of ways; the fingers were segmented to allow for flexibility, and that made for an odd sensation, in addition to the coolness of the metal … but at least the robot had agreed in its gentle, young woman's voice not to disclose this activity to anyone else.

Sometimes, when resentment became too strong, Amjad wondered if it would be possible to program Jimmy with an image of Basma's face. But it wasn't worth the risk, anyway, if Fadel were ever to stumble upon that in the maintenance robot's memory.

Whenever this bitterness accumulated, though, there was always a release waiting for Amjad that was better than any sex. At least Fadel hadn't exaggerated about that! It was the Merge … the one thing, in the end, that kept Amjad sane and afforded him an ongoing semblance of contentment.

Sometimes during his lunch hour, he'd gobble down his food quickly so he could spend most of that time Merging, and fortunately he had only run over his allotted hour on a few occasions, since his Merges seldom lasted more than twenty minutes. (Not forty minutes, on average, like damn perfect Fadel, but maybe his older brother was lying … always feeling the need to be superior.) Occasionally Amjad would sit in a men's room stall to Merge, soon enough becoming unaware of his coworkers coming and going, but there were only two stalls in each of the power plant's multiple restrooms so he felt it wasn't wise to tie them up, lest his coworkers lose patience with him. Therefore, he usually crawled into one of the maintenance chutes to Merge. He even Merged outside his lunchtime, when possible, if things were slow that shift. He could always lie and say he'd been doing such-and-such maintenance in there. Anyway, even if his team leader or supervisor didn't believe him, how much could they really chastise him when they were no doubt Merging at any opportunity, themselves … just like everyone else at Colony Hydra? In fact, he'd once let himself into his team leader's little office to ask him a question, only to find him with his head down on his desk, the little light at the back of his Merger glowing green.

On this day, with thankfully few duties to tend to between now and clock out, Amjad saw another opportunity to grab a Merge outside of his breaktime. He supposed that was one advantage to experiencing such short Merges, on average. And so, he made up a story to tell Jimmy about some cleanup he wanted to do in one of the chutes, in case anyone was looking for him.

"Would you like me to accompany you into the chute, Amjad?" Jimmy's default face, of a friendly-looking man in his forties, asked him pleasantly.

"Shh, no, not this time," Amjad said, glancing around to be sure no one had overheard them. He picked up his toolbox, to bring along with him as a useful visual prop. "I won't be in there too long."

And so, here he was now … nestled deep into the chute amongst some particularly thick bundles of cables, and hidden around the sharp right angle of a corner to boot. He had been sure to close the access panel behind him. He found it quite cozy in here, like an animal in its burrow, and the reactor's deep hum through the floor, walls, and ceiling of the dimly-lit duct were like a lullaby that would soon lull him into a soothing nothingness … so very far from his hungry body, his inadequate life … so very far removed from *everything*. From existence itself.

Though sometimes Fadel invited Amjad to come over for dinner at his apartment after their shift, that was surely not always the case, so no one noticed when Amjad didn't punch out for the evening. Fadel and Basma wouldn't be expecting him, and Amjad had no one waiting for him at his own little dorm room. Even his team leader didn't take note, too busy that day with some power fluctuations in the reactor room … where Amjad was not authorized to go. These spikes had recently been affecting the calibrated performance of the satellite dish, though some of the reactor room's technicians, including Fadel Idrissi, were perplexed and wondered if it wasn't the other way around: that the dish was somehow disturbing the functions of the reactor. After all, they *had* been steadily boosting power to the dish over time.

That is, no *human* noted Amjad's absence, but Jimmy did, since the automaton was the only worker Amjad had spoken to about venturing into one of the chutes to do some cleaning. Jimmy worked through all three shifts, though two of them amounted to little more than systems monitoring.

After the last workers of Amjad's shift trickled out of the power plant, and the members of the next shift settled in, Jimmy went to the chute into which Amjad had disappeared, opened its access panel, and peered inside.

"Amjad," it called, "are you still in there?"

No answer was forthcoming from back amongst those root-like clusters of cables, so after a few moments of indecision Jimmy climbed up through the opening … crawling forward on all fours.

Just ahead, where the chute took a right-hand turn, Jimmy spotted the edge of Amjad's toolbox poking out around the corner, having been set down there on the chute's green metal floor. Again, Jimmy called out, "Amjad? Are you all right? Did you fall asleep?" It wasn't unheard of for the workers to sometimes steal a nap in one of the warm ducts, if their shift was uneventful, especially on the two monitor shifts.

But as Jimmy turned the corner, the robot saw that Amjad wasn't stretched out asleep. Rather, Amjad—or the thing that had been a maintenance worker named Amjad Idrissi—sat in a ball-like position with its spiny backbone resting against one wall, its forked forelimbs wrapped around the front of its legs and its massive, spherical head resting on its knees, revealing how the Merger fused to the back of its head was mostly swallowed up by bone. The creature sat in a nest of what looked like blood-soaked blankets, which were in fact its shed clothing and flesh.

"Oh dear," Jimmy said. "I'll have to tell security about this."

But as if disrupted from its thoughts by the robot's words, the creature reared up its head … and then it was rapidly unfolding from its fetus-like position.

Before Jimmy could manage to scramble backwards, the corner and toolbox and bundled cables obstructing the move, the Amjad-creature seized the robot's head in its forelimbs, several of its talons catching themselves in the tight spaces between Jimmy's neck segments. Then, pulling back hard with all its strength, the creature sought to tear Jimmy's head from its root. All the while, the creature made clicking and popping sounds … jerking, wrenching, and twisting.

Jimmy tried to transmit a call for assistance, but in the end all it could do was emit a single, decidedly nonhuman squeal before its face screen fluttered and went mute. The dark-haired man's face expressed an approximation of distress, but wasn't capable of conveying true fear. Then, the screen showed only a blizzard of white static. Ultimately, even that was replaced with a blank silver plate, when Amjad finally tugged hard enough to dislodge the robot's head completely.

A sputter of bright sparks, accompanied by a wisp of smoke, and then the maintenance chute was dark and quiet once more.

-13-

Fuseli finally got back to his dorm room, to settle in for what was considered an evening … the Colony Hydra "day" being based on Earth's twenty-four hours and not on the tiny moon's ten-and-a-half-hour rotation. The first thing he did was use his wrist comp to put in a call to General Stroud, to get him up to speed on recent developments. In addition to Fuseli employing his device's scrambler, they also used an encrypted military channel.

"I don't know how many work shifts they have in the Plant," Fuseli told his commanding officer, "but while I was there I counted nine devices in the process of being assembled. There are supposedly only about a thousand Hydrans altogether, here and abroad. Even accounting for the need to replace children's units as they age, it looks like they're making more Mergers than they have people for. It's clear they plan on doing the primary thing cults do … recruit more cultists."

"Hm," Stroud said. "It's not like Gaithersburg hasn't been an interplanetary business all this time … but when it comes to implanting more people abroad, that's a whole other thing."

"Right. Along one wall they pointed out racks of shipping containers, supposedly to move the finished pieces to the med unit for Florence to implant … but those racks were *full* of containers. I'm sure most of what they're producing is going to go out on cargo ships, after those ships drop off supplies here. I bet it's already been underway for a while."

"Not illegal, of course," Stroud said, "but dangerous, if those contraptions are messing folks up." He drew in a long breath. "There are big politicians behind Colony Hydra, Bob … and not just Abbas. They court Gaithersburg for donation money, while Gaithersburg courts them for military contracts. Even I wasn't aware just how deep that relationship goes until recently."

"Like I say, the heads of the hydra don't all talk to each other," Fuseli said. "There are all kinds of factions in our government … even in the Colonial Forces."

"Well," Stroud sighed, "again, what the Hydrans are doing there isn't illegal, but—"

"But," Fuseli cut in, "if the health of Earth Colonies citizens is at risk, I strongly suggest we put a ban on the use of Mergers until the situation is better understood and the devices made safe—if they can be made safe."

"That's a tall order, Bob. There'd be all kinds of pushback from Congressman Abbas, which also means Gaithersburg, Incorporated."

"That's why it's not something I could do myself. All I can do is give my recommendation."

Stroud sighed again. "I'll … see what I can do about bringing that recommendation to the right ears."

"Sorry to be stirring up trouble again, sir," Fuseli said.

Stroud smiled. "Bob … why do you think I recommended you for this job in the first place? It sounded like a situation that needed someone who's not shy about turning over stones."

"I thought you told me not to ruffle any feathers."

"I knew you wouldn't listen."

Not long after he concluded his call with General Stroud, Fuseli heard his room's door buzz and he went to it. In the hallway outside he found Isobel Higgins, still wearing her charcoal business suit. She asked if she could come in, and he granted her access.

Once inside, she smiled and said, "I decided I'd offer you some personal help in your investigation, Bob … if it *can* be of any help to you."

"And what help would that be, Izzy?"

"I know you've been wanting to see someone actually in the process of Merging. It's still not looking good for Minister Abbas granting you access to the Ceremony Chamber during a group Merge, but I thought I'd offer to let you witness me doing an individual Merge."

Fuseli raised his eyebrows. "Oh! But I thought you said no one is allowed to witness a Merge who isn't Merging."

"I'm trying to be more open-minded, in the hopes that you will be, too."

"Well, I'm impressed by your offer, but I don't want you putting yourself at risk to help me. Seven people have already altered, and died as a result."

"Bob, whether you watch me or not, I'm still going to be doing individual Merges. I've done them countless times since I've lived at Colony Hydra. So you can witness my Merge … or I can just go retire to my flat now, and do it unobserved. The choice is yours."

Fuseli shrugged and wagged his head. "I don't know what it takes to get through to you people … "

"Please don't be insulting. I'm trying to help you, here."

"I'm only being *concerned*. So, does Abbas know you're offering to do this?"

"I haven't told anyone. This is between you and me."

"Then what can I say? If you're determined to do this anyway, I might as well watch. Maybe it could prove useful to me. But I'd prefer to have you do it in the med unit, where I can hook you up to monitors, and—"

"No … like I said, nobody knows I'm offering you this. I'd prefer to keep it that way, for now."

"All right, well, whatever. I have to do this on your terms."

"So you accept?" Her smile grew.

"Yes." He opened his arms wide. "So … how's this going to go?"

Izzy promptly slipped out of her suit jacket with its padded shoulders and draped it over the back of his desk's chair. Then, she reached up to her collar and unfastened it. It took Fuseli a couple of seconds to realize she had begun the process of fully removing her clothes. He watched as each article came away. She unfastened the side of her smooth, knee-length skirt and worked it down off her hips … stepped out of it. Soon she was down to only her bra and panties, and to Fuseli's surprise she removed even these articles and placed them neatly atop the folded pile of clothing she had placed on the chair's seat. Finished, she turned to him and smiled again.

"So," he said, "do you always strip down for the Merge? That guy Corrigan in the restroom today didn't do so."

"It depends on where you do it," Izzy stated, standing before him unabashedly. "Most of us prefer to be naked, to feel less connected to our bodies … more free of physical distractions. That's one of the reasons why we don't want witnesses to the group Merges. Outside the Ceremony Chamber there are lockers that everyone puts their clothes into before they go in. Everyone has to strip naked for the group Merge. We're afraid if people knew that, they'd think we were having these crazy orgies or something. It's a big circular chamber, and we all just lie down on our backs with our heads pointed toward the center, about a hundred of us at a time."

"I see. Thanks for giving me a better sense of things. And I appreciate you trusting me this way right now."

"We all want to see these deaths stop, as much as you might think we're nonchalant about it." Izzy gestured toward his bed. "May I?"

"Be my guest."

Izzy went to his bed, sat down on its edge and stretched out flat on her back with her arms at her sides. "Pull up a chair," she said.

Fuseli's flat had a second chair, besides the one occupied by her clothing, so he carried this closer to the bed and sat. "Now what?"

Her hair spread upon his pillow, Izzy looked up at him and said, "Please, just promise me you won't take any vids of me."

"Not even for my own use?"

She grinned. "Why do you need vids when you have the real thing right here … after I finish the Merge?"

"Well, the offers keep getting better, but I'm afraid I'm not in the position to accept it."

She made an exaggerated pout. "You could *get* into the position to accept it. Or any position of your choice."

Fuseli chuckled. "I have a lady in my life … and she'd kick my ass if she even knew I was seeing you in the nude right now."

"You *are* a doctor, though."

"It's best that we maintain that doctor-patient relationship."

"Your choice, Bob."

"You're killing me, Izzy."

She reached one hand to the back of her head, as she turned it to the side on his pillow for Fuseli to see her Merger. Her finger hovered over the device's only visible control: that tiny amber indicator light. "I guess we're ready to start, then."

"How long is this going to last?"

"I don't know. Sometimes there's no connection, though lately that's become less and less of a problem than in the past."

"Why do you think that is?"

"The satellite dish has been improved over time. It's become more sensitive."

"I see," said Fuseli. That sounded very significant to him, in terms of why these incidents of physical alteration were occurring only now, after the colony had existed here for seven years.

"Anyway, it might last anywhere from fifteen to forty minutes, for me. The average is about twenty." Her finger lightly rested on the amber indicator. "So … can I go ahead?"

"Go for it."

Izzy depressed and held the indicator for a count of three seconds, then released it. Fuseli saw it go green, before she rolled her head to face the ceiling again. She lowered her eyelids. "Here we go."

"How long does it take to—"

"*Shhh.*"

He didn't try speaking to her again, for fear of disrupting the process and causing some harm to her inadvertently. As he watched, the breathing through her nose deepened, her chest rising and falling slowly, as if she were willing herself into a trance.

Fuseli couldn't help but take in her body's pale skin, the tuft of curly, bright orange hair between her legs. He liked her human imperfections, such as the scattering of dark moles. Those cute ears. He wasn't one for cosmetic surgery. This was an uncomfortable position indeed, but he kept Rhan at the forefront of his mind. Once, he'd had a wife—in fact, he'd been married to Helena for almost two decades—but an affair with a nurse had helped kill that. He didn't want to hurt anyone like that again.

When after five minutes Izzy hadn't spoken to him again, he figured she'd achieved the mysterious state of Merging. Outwardly, without the benefit of proper equipment to monitor brain activity, he wasn't seeing anything noteworthy—beyond the obvious. Her eyelids fluttered ever so subtly, her lips had parted so that she now breathed through her mouth, but there was no shifting of limbs or twitching or any other movement from her body. If she was in something like a dream state, it was too early for REM sleep.

Twenty minutes came and went.

Still, Fuseli didn't speak to her, or even speak to himself aloud lest that break the spell. He scanned her as best he could within the limited abilities of his wrist comp's medical program, without touching her. Her heart rate was forty-five beats a minute, consistent with regular sleep. Twelve breaths per minute. Again, normal for a sleep state. Maybe the Hydrans only dreamed the Nought existed, after all, he thought … and it was all just a shared delusion. No other deep space probing system, except Gaithersburg's special dish and the servers that supported it, had ever detected "emanations" from that alleged alien race.

Thirty minutes. Forty.

Again, growing anxious, Fuseli moved his wrist comp close to her, without making contact, and took readings of her heart rate and respiration. They hadn't changed.

Fifty minutes.

Jesus, Izzy, he thought. He remembered that creature in the men's room hours earlier, cocking its head as if it had been struggling to understand his words … struggling to remember who it was, or had been.

Fifty-five minutes.

Perhaps she wasn't Merging, but had simply fallen asleep after a busy and upsetting day? He wanted to touch her shoulder, but didn't give in to the temptation.

At last, just a minute short of an hour, Izzy's eyelids began fluttering more noticeably, she drew in a few deeper breaths between her lips, and then her eyes cracked half open and she smiled at him dreamily.

"Hey there," he said.

"Hey, handsome."

"How was it?"

"Nice. That was a good, deep one. I'm very relaxed here with you."

"You had a long, tiring day."

"So did you. So … you saw how peaceful it was for me. I feel an afterglow like I can't even describe … a total sense of well-being. The only greater sense of well-being I can feel is when I'm in the Merge itself."

"Tell me about it. What you see."

"Nothing. I see nothing, I feel nothing. When the Merge is fully attained, there's just the wonderful emptiness of the void. The nothing at the center of everything. The *Nought*."

"And you say you don't speak with this race, or see through their eyes, or interact with them in any way?"

"Only in the sense that we feel a connection with them—a *connectedness* to them, and to each other when we're in a group. Though, I have to say, when you Merge singly like I did just now you get this funny, odd sense that you're connecting to one individual a little more than the rest. When you're together in a group, the sensation of communion is more diffused. But, stronger and more satisfying."

She sat up in his bed, swinging her bare legs over the edge to plant her feet on the floor. She held a hand out to him. He didn't know if she wanted him to help her stand up, or if she meant to pull him down beside her. *On* to her.

Instead, Fuseli got up from his chair, retrieved her folded clothing, and held it out to her upraised hand. "Oh well," she said, accepting the bundle. She stood up and stepped into her panties first. They were a satiny emerald green, but Fuseli took that to simply be a coincidence. No iridescent sheen, and they complemented her red hair. "You know, I'll say it again, Bob … the best way to understand is to try a Merger for yourself."

"Not a chance, Izzy."

"Not even to experience one, single Merge?"

"Not even that."

Izzy finished dressing, and slid her feet into her shoes. "Think about it, Bob."

He only grunted in answer, but then said, "Again, I thank you for letting me finally watch a Merge. I'm happy to say it was uneventful."

"You see? Totally benign. It isn't Merging that's harmful … it's some kind of virus or whatever in the *tool* with which we Merge."

"Possibly, but we've found no evidence of a virus yet."

Izzy started toward the door, but paused beside him and touched his hand. "I can come back here tomorrow night if you want … and stay next time."

"Good night, Izzy."

"Huh. Okay. Good night, Bob."

He watched her leave. When his door panel slid back in place, he went to it and punched the key to lock it. Then he stood there and thumped his forehead lightly against the panel twice.

"Rhan, Rhan, Rhan," he said. "It'll be good to get back to you."

-14-

Fuseli and Tarragon were just sitting down for coffee the next morning, so to speak, when Marco Zarate buzzed Fuseli on his wrist comp.

"I'm surprised your green-haired beauty let you out of bed this early, Mr. Zarate," he said.

"I couldn't wait to have a look at those circuitry sheets," the diagnostic tech said. "And the Merger that Florence removed from the latest corpse … uh, Corrigan. She delivered it here to the lab last night, while we were all sleeping."

"The pins," Fuseli said. "Were they of normal length?"

"Nope. They'd elongated, just like on the previous victim. Florence said they pierced his brain."

Fuseli looked up from the wrist comp's screen to meet Tarragon's eyes. "Now this sounds like a dangerous development indeed, if it's going to be a recurring thing. A boobytrap stuck to the skull of everybody in this colony." He didn't want to say it aloud just then, without their scramblers on—especially with colonists seated all around them in the cafeteria—but he needed to pass this information along to General Stroud, to help bolster the case for banning the devices.

"I haven't had a chance to look at the raw circuitry sheets yet, but I do have something exciting to show you, if you come down to the lab." In fact, Zarate's excitement was clear in his manner without him having to say it.

"We're on our way," Fuseli said, rising and taking his coffee to go.

"Okay, wait until you hear this!" Zarate gushed, as Fuseli and Tarragon stepped into his lab, coffees in hand. "They had some great translation programs to put at my disposal, but I still didn't expect to get anything from that body cam footage. Well, it took a while … I had to run the recording through like a thousand times … but I finally got it."

"You *did?*" Tarragon said.

"You haven't told anybody what you were up to, though, right?" Fuseli said. He and Tarragon had already activated their scramblers, but it was entirely possible that Zarate was being monitored at all other times in here. "Such as … your girlfriend?"

"Oh, she doesn't understand any of what I do, anyway."

"So Mikkelsen *was* speaking a language?"

"Yeah—a language that's never been encountered before! Listen to this." Zarate had recorded the translation of hydroponics farmer Jonas Mikkelsen's clicking, popping utterance onto his wrist comp, and he played it back for Fuseli and Tarragon now. The two military men leaned in closer to Zarate to listen carefully.

The audio extracted from Eva Gerling's helmet recording was raspy, unnatural, and reminded Fuseli of Security Chief Larck's translated voice, and yet what they heard was clearly words rendered into English.

"They pulled me out!" the voice hissed. Somehow the translation had even supplied an angry tone to the voice, despite its mechanical quality. *"Dislodged me from the Hive! I am only I again! I will kill them! Kill the invaders who set me adrift from the Hive!"*

"Jesus," Tarragon said under his breath.

"The Hive," Fuseli said. "That must be what the Hydrans call the Nought."

"A hive mind," said Tarragon. "Whatever consciousness Mikkelsen was connected to, it didn't like being disrupted."

"You heard it," Fuseli said. "It said *invaders.* What the Hydrans are doing, reaching out to them, interfacing with their hive mind … the Nought see it as invasive."

"Or maybe just some of them feel that way?" Zarate suggested. "Because this mutation thing isn't happening to all the Hydrans."

"Not yet," said Fuseli. "Send me that file. I need to play this recording for Abbas and his cabinet. They need to know that the Nought don't seem to feel the same way about the Merge as the Hydrans do."

Fuseli called Abbas on his wrist comp and stressed that he needed to meet with the Head Minister immediately. Abbas told him he was presently in a meeting—whether that was with the colony's lesser ministers or with the board of directors of Gaithersburg, Incorporated, it didn't make a difference, the individuals in question being the same thing—but he expected to be free in about an hour.

"I suggest you have everybody stay in the conference room for when I get there," Fuseli told him. "They should all hear what I have to share."

After a weighted pause, perhaps wary of Fuseli's tone, Abbas said, "I'll do that."

While he waited, Fuseli decided to go have a look at the latest altered corpse to come into the med unit. He was actually more interested, though, in having a few words with Florence. Tarragon accompanied him.

When Fuseli got there, Florence promptly opened the cryo chamber drawer in which the body of Bryce Corrigan was being preserved. Staring down at it, Fuseli said to the robot, "You should have waited until I had a chance to examine the body before removing the Merger for Mr. Zarate."

"My apologies, Dr. Fuseli," said the automaton. "Next time I'll be sure to wait."

"*Next* time?" Tarragon said. "God forbid."

"I took the liberty of running a series of scans myself," said the robot. Stepping over to a nearby monitor screen, Florence called up an interior scan of Corrigan's transformed body, and pointed a metallic finger. "Though alterations to the internal organs have generally not progressed, deformations to the brain appear to have increased in this subject, along with the severity of external changes to his body. As you can see, there are oddities involving the meninges between the brain and cranium. These thin growths here, in the pia mater, I at first took for blood vessels … but they're actually new nerve structures, proceeding through the dura mater and even through the cerebrospinal fluid, to connect with the inner surface of the bone itself."

"Again," Fuseli said, "this makes me think the skull is being turned into some kind of sensory organ, if not quite an eye."

"It could well be," Florence said.

Fuseli switched his attention from the bizarre corpse to the robot's face, which watched him with its avatar's attractive if empty eyes. "I want to ask you some questions, Florence. No matter how you may have been programmed by these people, I trust you to tell me the truth more readily than any of them."

"Perhaps you're judging the colonists too harshly, Doctor."

"Just be quiet and listen. Klaus Gaithersburg died four years ago, while living here at the colony. Correct?"

"Yes, Doctor."

"So you had to have tended to him when he was dying … or examined his body after death, at least."

"Yes. Both Dr. Sung and I examined Mr. Gaithersburg's body when it was discovered that he had passed."

"I asked Isobel Higgins how he died, and she seemed evasive. Tell me what you and Dr. Sung found to be the cause."

Florence hesitated for a second, but that was as far as the machine went in being evasive, itself. "Mr. Gaithersburg was determined to have died of a ruptured brain aneurysm."

Fuseli nodded in satisfaction. He'd had an intuition. "So … he was actually the *first* of these victims, wasn't he?"

Florence held up a cautioning finger. "Not quite, Doctor. Mr. Gaithersburg suffered no alterations to his body or brain, such as we've seen in these seven victims … not to mention the passing of three years in which there were no other strange deaths."

"Okay, but do you at least attribute his death to his use of a Merger?"

Again, that single beat of hesitation. "Yes," Florence said flatly.

"Explain."

"Mr. Gaithersburg attempted to adjust the sensitivity of his own device, to increase its connection with the race he had named the Nought. It … turned out to have been an ill-advised experiment to perform on himself. Perhaps his age had to do with his lapse in judgment."

"Or maybe," Tarragon said, "he knew he didn't have too many years left ahead of him anyway, and wasn't afraid to take the risk."

"For a businessman," Florence said, "he had a great commitment to the advancement of science."

"For a scientist," Fuseli said, "he had a great commitment to hoarding his discoveries for his own little community."

"His company continues to share many useful, innovative products with the public to this day," Florence countered.

"Okay, so he also had a great commitment to making money. Anyway … tell me all you, personally, know about the Nought. And yes, I understand, you're an outsider—you haven't experienced the Merge yourself, and you can't. But tell me what you've learned living here … I mean, in your time here. You're a doctor, despite what you say. People open up to doctors … and not just their bodies."

Florence didn't speak for more than just a second this time, so Tarragon cut in. "Your very existence is to ensure the safety of these colonists. It's your *duty* to tell us anything we need to know that can help us keep them alive."

"I don't truly have a sense of duty, Lieutenant Tarragon," Florence said, "but I do have programming, and I am indeed programmed to ensure the health and well-being of the Hydrans. Tell me what you need to know."

"First, in clinical terms—no blissed-out rhapsodizing," Fuseli said. "What is it exactly they're doing when they Merge?"

"On their world," Florence said, "or perhaps in some pocket universe of their own creation, the race the Hydrans call the Nought seem to spend the whole of their existence in a state of linked unconsciousness. They may even no longer possess physical bodies. It was Klaus Gaithersburg's belief that the Nought had once been a brutally violent race … that through many generations of war and tribalism they had nearly extinguished themselves. He felt this communal state of mind they finally achieved was the salvation of their species. No more factions, no more divisions along economic or racial lines … everyone linked, no one in a greater position of power than anyone else. Beyond material concerns and personal possessions. They cast it all away … until all that was left was a great *nothing*."

"Nothing became their God," Tarragon said.

"It's believed the Nought are beyond mere atheists," Florence said. "They don't embrace the absence of a god so much as embrace the absence of conscious existence. The Hydrans feel they've learned from this lesson, and that by following the Nought's example humans, too, can ultimately transcend conflict and hatred. The colonists claim that in experiencing the Merge, they have attained the ultimate state of peace … if only for an hour at a time. I've heard the Merge described as a temporary death. It's the freedom of becoming dead … except that one is returned to life afterward, only to look forward to the next death. And the next."

"And yet," Fuseli said, "paradoxically, the Hydrans—and presumably the Nought—seem to experience a sense of *wholeness* when they're all linked together like that. A kind of fullness and an emptiness at the same time."

"As you say, Doctor, it's difficult for me to fathom, being an outsider to the experience. All I can do is repeat what others have said … what Mr. Gaithersburg himself said, sometimes even in my presence. That the Nought have advanced to a state of complete unity, in which they allow themselves to sleep a dreamless sleep … a bubble adrift on the sea of an eternal and infinite void."

"And yet," Fuseli said, "I now have evidence to suggest that as much as the Hydrans may want to cut in on that dance—to insinuate themselves into the Nought's hard-won state of peace—the Nought might not care for that intrusion. Might, in fact, bitterly resent it."

-15-

As soon as he'd begun the day's shift in the power plant's Reactor Control Center, Fadel Idrissi had been greeted with the news that the third shift had been keeping their eye on some unusual power spikes that had increased over the past few hours.

The control room was contained in one of the largest of Colony Hydra's structures: a great dome of solid green metal, dwarfing the colony's hydroponics domes. Its interior was thus circular, ringed with work stations manned by humans and robots alike, and at the center of this chamber was an observation bay of windows that looked down into the subterranean reactor chamber itself. Of course, the reactor was shielded in a thick protective capsule, but fixed cameras and even hovering drones within that casing gave the control room's technicians a view of its interior, beyond the information supplied by the countless monitors and gauges that filled their work stations. Currently Fadel sat in front of some of these monitors, both physical and holographic, and frowned at the readings they displayed.

Actually, Fadel been monitoring power fluctuations with the reactor for several weeks, but today's spikes were a bit concerning. A number of his screens flashed orange, to indicate readings were in the caution zone. No red screens, or warning klaxons, yet … but he was almost ready to worry about the possibility.

A coworker named Marta leaned over his shoulder, to study the readings along with him. "The increase to the dish we implemented yesterday might be throwing things off … causing feedback. Though I haven't noticed a loop pattern yet."

"From the looks of things, I'm thinking the same," said Fadel. "Random surges. Unpredictable … but feeding back from the dish."

"Maybe we should dial its power down a little?"

"Maybe, but I'd want to check with Minister Abbas himself before we did anything like that. He always wants us inching forward … not falling back."

"Well, when you inch to the edge of a volcano you might just *have* to back off a bit. If there was too much of a power surge, and it routed to the Merger Control Room, it might cook every brainframe in the servers … and I know Minister Abbas would not like *that*."

"None of us would," Fadel muttered, reaching out to flick through different data readouts. Meanwhile, one of his screens displayed a floating drone's-eye-view of the reactor from inside its sarcophagus, but from here nothing concerning appeared to be going on. At least not externally. "We'll watch for major flare-ups to see that they're routed safely. That's priority one. Ground any lightning strikes, so to speak."

"I'd say priority one is making a call to Minister Abbas," Marta mumbled, but mostly to herself. Fadel was a senior engineer, not a mere tech like herself. Still, she couldn't help but add, "There's also the threat of the core overheating."

Gruffly, he reminded her, "Coolant will compensate automatically if the core starts to overheat. We'll balance this shit out and settle things down."

Another tech poked his head into the Reactor Control Room. "Hey," the young man called out, "has anyone seen that damn robot Jimmy?"

"Not in here," Marta called back to him.

"Maybe he's charging?" the young tech suggested. "Or did someone take him to the shop for some work … an upgrade or something?"

"We don't have time to worry about where Jimmy is!" Fadel snapped. "We're busy in here!"

"Sorry … sorry." The young tech withdrew and closed the control room's door again.

"Please, baby," Fhuum purred, tracing the outside of Zarate's ear with one long-nailed finger. Salon worker that she was, she'd painted her fingernails and toenails an iridescent green. "*Please.*"

They lay together in his bed, and she had stripped him of all his clothes herself. She'd even removed his wrist comp, shut it off, and wrapped it up in the bundle of his shirt. One of her long legs was hooked over one of his, and that skin-on-skin was a wonderful sensation, but it would be a little while before Zarate had the energy for another round with her.

"I really should be getting back to my lab, sweetie," he told her. "I shouldn't even be here right now." Despite being told not to go to Zarate's lab, she had done just that … and dragged him here to his room. He hadn't resisted all that much. "Later tonight we can—"

"Oh come *on*, baby," Fhuum said, "you work too hard. You deserve a break. Let's just do this thing, and you can go right back to work afterwards. I swear, you need zero recovery time."

"But … I don't know, hon," Zarate said, wincing. "I mean, if you saw those fucking mutated bodies up close like I have … "

"I *know* it's horrible; I knew those people myself! I mean, I wasn't close to any of them, but … " She leaned in with her face, and her broad tongue emerged from her wide Choom mouth to slowly lick Zarate along the line of his jaw. Then she said, "But this would be a brand new one, right off the line. State of the art! And I swear, if you don't like it, after you give it an honest try you can have it pulled off just like that." She snapped her fingers. "Just as fast as Florence puts it in."

Zarate sighed. "Hon … I'm really excited about what Gaithersburg does, all its incredible tech, and I'd honestly like to try it … *truly* I would … but waiting until after we've absolutely figured out what's going on here would make me a hell of a lot more comfortable."

"Fine." Abruptly, Fhuum swung her leg off his, sat up on the edge of the bed, and got to her feet. Naked, her long green hair spilling down her slender back, she stomped over to where she'd scattered her clothing across his dorm room's green carpet. "Maybe I'll just stay away from you, and let you help those asshole Colonial Forcers harass poor Minister Abbas … so I don't distract you. Then, if you ever feel less afraid to do what every man, woman, and fucking *child* in Colony Hydra has been brave enough to do … maybe *then* you can come see me again." With that, she stepped into her skimpy panties, working them up her hips and their thong strap between her buttocks.

"Honey … wait, come on," Zarate implored her, sitting up in bed, too, and reaching out for her with one hand. "Don't go—please."

She scowled at him as she tugged up her form-fitting tights. "You don't trust us. You don't trust *me*. Even after I've let you watch me Merge, and you saw how peaceful it is. And here you told me you were thinking about moving to Hydra, and working for Gaithersburg yourself … making tons of money. Did you say all that just so I'd keep sleeping with you?"

"No, no, no!" Zarate insisted, springing out of bed and rushing to her desperately, taking her by the arms. "I *did* mean all that! I mean … I meant that I was thinking about it!"

"Well, how could you ever become a colonist here if you didn't let yourself be implanted … *huh?* No one here isn't implanted; not a single solitary soul, unless they're a *baby!*"

Zarate sighed, rubbing his thumbs against her inner elbows, his face pained. "Hon, don't talk like you're going to stop seeing me. I don't want to lose you! You're the best thing that's ever happened to me!"

Fhuum cupped his face in her hands, and stroked his cheeks with her own thumbs. "I want us to stay together, baby, but that's all up to you! It's all *your* choice. But if you love me like you say, and trust me like I thought you did, then come with me now … to the med unit. To see Florence. We don't need any kind of clearance, any kind of permission. Only your own consent."

"But … but maybe I should tell Captain Fuseli first."

Fhuum's eyes narrowed and she jerked her hands away from his face. "He'll tell you no. He'll forbid it. But maybe that's what you want … you *want* him to forbid it, so you don't have to make the decision for yourself."

"No, sweetie, no … that's not it!" His grip tightened on her arms a bit, but not roughly.

"You work for the Earth Colonies, but not for the Colonial Forces. You aren't military. You don't need that miserable asshole's permission. You only need your *own* permission. But if you do it, Marco, do it for yourself. Not even for me—*yourself.* If you experience the Merge just once, I know you'll never regret it. None of us do! Why do you think we're still Merging even with these anomalies happening? And that's all they are—random anomalies." She now looked to be on the verge of tears as she gave this impassioned speech. "Marco, it's because I love you that I want you to feel the freedom I feel! I want you to know the ultimate sense of peace, just like me … just like the rest of us! Then, baby, you and I will truly be together. We'll be *one*, in a relationship more intimate than fucking, more intimate than marriage. We'll be *Merged.*"

Zarate's eyes had filled with tears, as well, but a smile cracked his face then under his bushy mustache … a smile almost as great as a Choom's. "Okay, honey," he whispered. "Okay. Take me to Florence."

Because the servers that dominated the Merger Control Center generally only needed to be monitored as they went about their deeply humming work, the room was usually only manned by one robot, with the face of an elderly Asian man as its default avatar, and one human worker. On this shift, that human was Arseny Golov.

When there wasn't much to do, which was most of the time, Arseny and the robot—called Atsushi—played chess on an actual physical board, and Arseny prided himself on sometimes winning. Today, though, the systems were demanding a little more attention from both of them, as some significant power spikes had shown on their monitors. After the last spike, more dramatic than anything he'd seen to date, Arseny had called to report it to the reactor room, in its dome up there on the moon's surface. A tech named Marta had answered and assured him they were watching the situation and had everything under control.

Arseny wasn't put too much at ease by that predictable assertion, especially since Marta hadn't sounded too convinced herself, but all he could do was trust that those with more expertise and higher standing than himself did in fact know what they were doing. Then again, the great Klaus Gaithersburg had felt he knew what he was doing … and look where pushing things too far had got *him*.

Atsushi was presently on the side of the control center nearest the entrance, out of view behind the long rows of servers, seated at one of the monitoring stations. Arseny was on the far side of the room, recording figures from a series of readouts into his wrist comp—as he was required to do once an hour—when he heard a strange, hollow clunking sound up by the ceiling.

Arseny paused from his notations to turn and look in that direction. Sure enough, another hollow, metallic bang followed, further along than the first. It sounded to him as if someone was moving through the access chute behind the wall, where bundles of cables that branched off from the power plant snaked underground to feed such departments as the Plant and the Merger Control Center itself.

Arseny moved closer to the wall in question, and there he thought he heard a subtler but consistent scraping sound inside the wall, as if someone in the chute was crawling along and dragging a metal toolbox.

Stepping over to the access panel above his head, which was there to permit entry into the conduit, Arseny said, "Hey … somebody in there? That you, Santa Claus?"

No one answered, but the scraping sound stopped, as if whoever was in the chute had paused to listen to him.

"Are you switching out some cables?" Arseny asked. "You afraid these spikes are going to fry the servers?"

Still no response, but the scraping progress through the duct didn't continue. Arseny swore someone was directly behind that access panel, but why weren't they responding? Could it be whoever it was wasn't supposed to be in there, and they were afraid they'd been caught? Were waiting until Arseny lost interest so they could proceed again? It wouldn't be one of those people who'd come to investigate matters here, would it? That diagnostic tech sneaking around? What was his name … Zarate?

"Hello?" Arseny said, his tone now grown impatient. "I know you're there, Santa Claus."

The ceiling in here wasn't all that high, the server banks nearly touching it. However, to reach the brainframe drawers slotted into the servers near the top, the workers still kept on hand a mobile metal stepladder on rollers. The stepladder was nearby, so Arseny went to it, rolled it over to the access panel, then locked the wheels to keep the thing secure when he climbed it. Then, Arseny mounted the corrugated metal steps and reached to the access panel.

"I don't know why you won't answer," he said, as he opened it. "Trying to sneak a peek at—"

As Arseny Golov inserted his head into the chute, it was immediately grasped by four hook-tipped forelimbs. One talon pierced an eyeball and caught against the inside of the skull socket. Two other claws, in yanking Arseny's entire body through the access panel and into the chute beyond, even ripped the man's Merger half out of his head, three of its pins coming free.

Arseny tried to scream, but the thing that had been Amjad Idrissi leaned over him and seized his throat in its four tooth-lined mouthparts … clamping down hard.

As the access panel swung back into place on its own, and Amjad tore out his throat, Arseny tried kicking the chute's walls in the hope of alerting Atsushi. But in only seconds, instead of kicking he was merely sliding his heels feebly in the stream of blood that flowed out of him, and along the floor of the chute.

-16-

Arranged around the conference room's long table, Rusul Abbas and the twelve other ministers sat in silence as they absorbed the translation Marco Zarate had finally produced from the sounds made by Jonas Mikkelsen. Fuseli had just played the recording for them from his wrist comp, and he himself was not seated … instead paced around the room as he spoke. Tarragon stood against one wall, arms folded. Against the opposite wall, behind Abbas, stood Security Chief Larck. Two of Larck's security people flanked the door. Isobel Higgins also had a place at the table. On his way here from the med unit, Fuseli had tried calling Zarate to have him join them, as well, so as to explain how he'd managed to extract the translation, but the man hadn't answered.

"Not random sounds," Fuseli said as he stalked the room, "but an alien language. What you're hearing—for the first time, despite your seven years here Merging with the Nought—is one of them speaking in their own words. Expressing how they *feel* about your Merge."

One of the ministers protested, "Those words could be interpreted—"

Fuseli broke in before the man could finish. "Interpreted another way? What could be vague about this?" And he played the recording a second time.

"They pulled me out! Dislodged me from the Hive! I am only I again! I will kill them! Kill the invaders who set me adrift from the Hive!"

"Dislodged me," Fuseli repeated. "I am only *I* again … "

"Where is Mr. Zarate?" Abbas asked. "I'd like to hear him explain, himself, how he made this recording."

"I'll try him again," Tarragon said, turning his attention to his own wrist comp.

"The meaning here," Fuseli said, "couldn't be more clear, especially in light of the behavior we've seen from every one of the seven transformed victims. Violent behavior, that so far has resulted in the murder of Dr. Zhen Sung, and the injury of several others."

The minister Fuseli remembered as Moussa said, "You're suggesting malign intent from the Nought themselves … we get it. But in the end, that was one of our colonists speaking … a human of Earth origin named Jonas Mikkelsen. Those sentiments he expressed, as best he could in his physically altered condition, were his own. That's why our technology was able to translate him. All of these victims are not in their right mind, and who can blame them if their fear and pain causes them to lash out in violence?"

"Exactly," said Sonya, who had toured the Plant with Fuseli and the others the day before. "What Jonas said about being dislodged … set adrift. He's expressing his frustration at not being able to Merge. Merging brings a profound sense of peace, which in those moments Jonas was certainly *not* feeling. It isn't one of the Nought who's speaking there, through Jonas, but only the poor man himself."

"You're being willfully blind," Fuseli argued. "*Invaders*, he said."

"Dr. Fuseli … " the woman went on.

Fuseli started reading names off his wrist comp as he continued pacing the room behind the seated cabinet members. "Lalita Begum … she was the first victim. Died from the alterations to her body. Lootan Habuul … second victim, a Choom. Died from alterations to her body. Third victim, Naresh Gupta, died from alterations to his body … "

"We know who we've lost," said Moussa, "all too well!"

Fuseli ignored him. "Fourth victim, Vardon Grigoryan. Shot by a security guard after he'd killed Dr. Zhen Sung. Fifth victim, Josef Elmi … killed by me. Sixth victim, Jonas Mikkelsen, killed by Security Chief Larck. Seventh victim, Bryce Corrigan, killed by Lieutenant Tarragon." Fuseli stopped pacing, confronting Abbas directly. "Do you know what they all had in common? It's that they all changed after they had Merged in private. Not in your group Merge, in the Ceremony Chamber. They had Merged *singly*."

"And?" Moussa said, slapping a hand onto the table.

"Do you think we haven't noticed that pattern ourselves, Captain

Fuseli?" Abbas said. He was maintaining his outward cool better than Moussa, but his eyes smoldered.

"It's my understanding," Fuseli went on, not allowing himself to betray Izzy with a look as he said this, "that when you Merge on your own like that, you sometimes feel a connection with an individual Nought, rather than the entire hive mind."

"*Some* of us have had a vague sense of that," Abbas replied. "It isn't something all of us experience, at all times."

"Neither do you all experience these physical alterations, but it still happens."

"What is your point?"

"My point is, that you people are hijacking the Nought's own state of Merging. You're … colonizing it. Maybe they're so deep in that state they don't even acknowledge that you're doing it … may not even be aware of you … because your connection with them is diffused across the whole. But when *one* of you connects to the Hive, as they call it, it sometimes causes a connection with a single entity in that group, and it crudely disrupts them."

For a third time, he played the recording. *"They pulled me out! Dislodged me from the Hive! I am only I again! I will kill them! Kill the invaders who set me adrift from the Hive!"*

Fuseli continued, "It was Klaus Gaithersburg's feeling that the Nought were once been a savage, bloodthirsty race that nearly brought about their own destruction … correct?"

"Who told you that?" Moussa demanded.

"How did Gaithersburg glean that insight?" Fuseli asked. "By gradually boosting his own Merger's power, trying to learn more and more from them? Until those adjustments finally killed him?"

Moussa jumped up from his seat, eyes bulging in a face of rage. "What do you think you know?"

"The Nought don't welcome your communion with them. When they become aware of it, it *angers* them. You're interfering in their existence … stealing from them. But when this intrusion *really* interferes is when a link is made between two individuals, and one of them is woken from its sleep of nothingness, and its consciousness is dragged here against its will … into an alien body."

"Stop!" Moussa shouted. He turned helplessly to Abbas. "Minister, please, don't let him speak such—"

"*Blasphemies?*" Fuseli said. "You know it's true; you may have figured all this out already. I don't think you even *care* whether the Nought resent the Merge or not, so long as you get what you want from it. Meanwhile, people on their end are getting pried out of the Hive. Trapped in a human body, confused and afraid and angry. Either consciously or unconsciously, this individual Nought exerts its will over the host body to reform it into a more recognizable self-image. But the changes are more external than internal, for the most part, because when we visualize ourselves of course we don't envision our internal organs, and neither do they. And anyway, leaving the human internal organs mostly unchanged makes for a more viable lifeform, for our environment."

"And how do you think they accomplish these changes," Sonya asked, "if it's the Nought doing that, and not some fault with the Mergers? Through *magic?*"

"They must be highly advanced beings, with powerful mental capabilities beyond our understanding."

"You'll say anything to support your own prejudices against us," Moussa snarled. "You just want to take your slanderous opinions about our community back to our enemies!"

"Your enemy is the *truth*," Fuseli said. "Why do you think every victim is becoming more and more outwardly changed, but following a consistent model? Are you going to tell me that's not what the Nought looked like, back when they still lived their lives in the physical world? When they were still those bloodthirsty, war-like beings? Beings that you're forcing them to revert into?"

"Enough!" Murgan Larck rumbled in his own translated voice, taking a step forward and pointing a clawed finger at Fuseli. "I caution you to stand down, Captain. You won't speak to these government officials that way."

Fuseli drew in a long breath. Maybe he was going a little too far, too fast, but then again General Stroud had finally admitted he'd sent him here to flip stones over. At least he hadn't revealed the recommendation he'd given to Stroud, that the use of Mergers should be officially banned by the Earth Colonies. Instead, he said, "Minister Abbas, if you and your people insist on continuing to use these devices while my investigation is still underway, at the very least you have to tell your people to stop Merging individually … outside of the ceremony group. If you're afraid they won't obey such an order, surely you could find a way to block or shut down everyone's Merger except when they're in the Ceremony Chamber."

"Out of the question!" said Moussa, and other ministers were wagging their heads strongly in the negative.

"Our people would never consent to that," Abbas stated.

"Don't ask for their consent. It's for their own good."

"Listen to this man!" Moussa said, astonished. "Don't ask for our people's consent?"

"Do you ask the children's consent before you bolt those contraptions to their heads?" Fuseli snapped.

"Captain … " Larck said, taking an ominous step away from the wall. In response, Tarragon also took one step forward, his gaze locked on the Gurm.

"Captain Fuseli," Abbas said, "I thank you for your efforts here … I know you mean well. However, I think it was a mistake to bring you to Colony Hydra. Our community boasts many skilled people in many diverse fields, and I believe we can go forward from here without your involvement."

Fuseli shook his head and smiled. "I'm sorry, Congressman, but I have an assignment to fulfill, and now that I'm here I'm required by my commanding officer to do that. I take my orders from the Colonial Forces."

"Then I suppose I must contact your General Stroud, with your

Colonial Forces, and tell him I would prefer you be ordered to leave my colony."

"You may certainly do that, sir. I'm sure he'd give it his consideration."

"In the meantime, I don't see how you can expect to help us here, when you hold our community in such contempt."

"I'm not motivated by contempt," Fuseli said, as he started toward the conference room's door. "I'm just a doctor … doing his job."

At that, he left the conference room, briefly meeting Izzy's eyes on the way out. He couldn't read her expression, except that she wasn't smiling.

Tarragon trailed him out of the room. Over his shoulder, Fuseli asked, "Still couldn't get a hold of that damn Zarate, to come back me up a little?"

"No luck with that, Captain," Tarragon said.

-17-

On his way back to his dorm room, Fuseli opened a channel on his wrist comp to call General Stroud and let him know about his confrontation with Abbas and the other cabinet ministers. However, he couldn't get a call out. He and Tarragon stopped in the middle of the hallway in which they'd been walking while Fuseli tried several other channels, but he found all of them were as good as dead. Nothing but static.

"Let me try mine," Tarragon said, but Fuseli could tell from his tone that he didn't expect any success. His suspicions were correct. "Fuckers are blocking communications. They didn't waste any time, did they? Abbas must have called somebody the minute we stepped out the door."

"Are they blocking just us, or are they playing it safe and shutting down the whole colony?"

"Let's find somebody and borrow their wrist comp and see." Tarragon looked around them and spotted a young couple, maybe not even out of their teens, strolling around the corner and into the dormitory hallway in which they stood. Tarragon whistled to them and gestured for the couple to come to him. They froze up for a moment, plainly afraid, but obeyed the huge Black man's summons.

Up close, it was more apparent that they were teenagers. "Yes, sir?" the boy said meekly.

"Let me see if I can get a call out on your comp," Tarragon said to the girl, as the boy didn't wear one. Hers wasn't the most expensive model, but it should have the basic functions. "Mine isn't working," Tarragon added. The girl extended her arm and watched as the Colonial Forcer fiddled with her device, and Fuseli stepped closer to watch as well. However, no communications channel was able to transmit, or apparently receive, either.

"How does that bastard think he's going to get away with this?" Fuseli fumed.

"He's desperate," Tarragon said. "Feeling the heat now." Tarragon let go of the girl's arm and nodded at her. "You can run along."

As the couple quickened their pace to escape the camo-uniformed soldiers, Fuseli said, "He'll probably try blaming this on a communications outage, but he can't keep Colony Hydra in the dark forever. What's he going to do now? These people know when we share what we've learned, especially from that recording, it's going to discredit the hell out of this whole Gaithersburg cult."

"Let's get back to your dorm," Tarragon said, "and I'll copy that recording onto my comp, too, in case they try frying yours remotely. The more copies the better."

"Speaking of the recording," Fuseli said, "we should stop by Zarate's lab first. Since the dumbass wouldn't answer our calls—back when we could still make calls. I want to secure his original recording … and Eva Gerling's helmet, too. It's still in there."

"Good idea," said Tarragon. "Let's go."

Fuseli found the door to Zarate's lab unlocked, which he took to mean Zarate was inside … but when the door panel slid open it wasn't the diagnostic tech he saw inside, but four Colonial Forcers in full black garb, with full-head black helmets. One of them held an extra black helmet in their gloved hands: that of Corporal Eva Gerling.

The other three C-Forcers spun around with Drangs gripped in their fists, leveled at Fuseli. Nevertheless, rather than duck back into the corridor and punch the door control to get it closed again, he stepped forward into the room. Slipping in ominously behind him, hand on the grip of his holstered pistol, came Tarragon.

"Put that helmet back down, soldier," Fuseli said.

"Sorry, sir," came the voice of a female C-Forcer over her own helmet's mic.

"You're to come with us, sir," said another of the soldiers, without lowering his formidable assault engine with its multiple deadly functions. Though it could fire tranquilizer darts, Fuseli doubted these security members would resort to nonlethal measures if it came down to fighting two Special Ops soldiers.

"You'd better quit pointing those weapons at my captain," Tarragon rumbled.

"Give me that helmet," Fuseli said. "That's a direct order."

"Sorry, sirs," the one holding Gerling's helmet said again. "We're on orders from the Head Minister."

"I told you they're Colonial Forcers in name only," Tarragon said to Fuseli.

One of the soldiers slung his Drang around to his side on its strap, and produced a pair of hand restraints. He took a step closer to Fuseli warily. "Please place your hands behind your back, Captain."

"Are you kidding me, soldier? Where do you intend to take me?"

"If we were to spot you, we were to hold you for Chief Larck, sir. He'll answer your questions."

Fuseli and Tarragon looked at each other gravely, their eyes exchanging the next best thing to telepathy. Could they overwhelm these four soldiers with force? If Fuseli were to grab the one with the cuffs when he got close enough, he could use the man as a shield, while Tarragon pulled his handgun. The one with the helmet had her hands occupied, so that left two with Drangs aimed at them … but maybe they'd be afraid to fire, for fear of hitting their captured friend. And maybe they'd be too afraid to fire on Colonial Forces officers, after all, despite their threatening demeanor. But ultimately, the risk that they would indeed open fire was too great … and Fuseli didn't think he and his friend would get out of this room alive, anyway, without having to kill at least a couple of these soldiers, and that he didn't want to have to do.

"Let's go see what our boy Larck wants to say," Fuseli said to Tarragon, reaching both hands behind his back and turning to offer them to the man with the cuffs.

Tarragon hesitated; not that he was considering disobeying a superior officer, as these others were doing, but only to convey his displeasure. Then he too put his hands behind his back, and offered himself to the one who had just secured Fuseli. As the man first removed his wrist comp, as he had done with Fuseli, Tarragon said to him, "I don't know who you four grunts are by name, so I'm going to personally recommend every last C-Forcer on this moon for a dishonorable discharge. You hear that, you brainwashed little traitor?"

"Yes, sir," said the man adjusting his cuffs to fit Tarragon's wrists. "Sorry, sir."

Lastly, the man who had handcuffed the two officers took the Scythe handguns from their holsters.

"Did you already take Zarate prisoner?" Fuseli asked, as the soldiers began marching him and Tarragon out into the corridor.

"No, sir," said the woman carrying the helmet. "But he's in good hands."

There must not be much in the way of crime at Colony Hydra, because the two Special Ops men found that the security office to which they were brought contained only a single cell to serve as the brig. Fuseli and Tarragon were uncuffed and directed to go inside, but first a combat knife sheathed in the outside of Tarragon's right boot was confiscated, as well. As the man took it, Tarragon purred, "I don't need that … I could twist your head off with my bare hands, mister."

The cell's door panel slid into place and clunked heavily as it locked. The cell itself contained two benches of the same green alloy as the rest of the tiny room, with thin mattresses and no blankets. Between the benches stood a toilet with the tank doubling as a sink. Also green.

"I never want to see the color green again after this," Fuseli said, as he and Tarragon each took a bench, sitting to face each other.

"I'll bet they sent other teams to our dorm rooms," Tarragon said. "Soon as we left that meeting, Larck must have put all his people on the lookout for us. But what are they going to do … kick us off Hydra? And then what? They think there'll be no repercussions?"

"Congressman Abbas with all his connections will say that damn Captain Fuseli, with his reputation for stirring up trouble, was out of line … threatened the security of an Earth Colonies settlement. Threatened the operations of an important corporation. Suchlike bullshit."

"Or maybe they'll just … make us disappear," Tarragon said.

"That's a bit much, Morris."

"These *people* are a bit much, Captain. You've said it yourself, and it couldn't be more true: they're a cult. They could take us out in any number of ways. Claim we were killed by one of those mutants. Killed by a radiation leak in Zarate's lab. They might have to kill him, too, to claim something like that … if they haven't killed him already."

"Congressman or not, if we were to end up dead you know General Stroud would be all over that bastard. Abbas underestimates the Colonial Forces. The ones who haven't been turned into zombies for him, anyway."

"That won't be much consolation to us if we're dead."

The two men looked up as they saw a familiar figure step up to the window in the cell's locked door. Peering in at them was the turquoise-scaled, lizard-like face of Security Chief Murgan Larck.

"This is a most unfortunate situation, gentlemen," came his translated voice, over the cell's speaker. "But here we are."

Fuseli rose from his bench and moved close to the door. "You will face a court martial, Sergeant Larck, I hope you know that. Your whole history as a gunship pilot in the Gurm Conflict … all your accomplishments … besmirched. You'll be disgraced."

"I'm only following orders, Captain."

"The only orders you should be following are *mine*. Where's Abbas now? Too cowardly to face me in person?"

"The cabinet is discussing what comes next. I'm just to hold you until they figure that out."

"I can't believe a proud Gurm warrior would even join a cult like this in the first place. That thing on your head must be a hell of a drug, Sergeant."

After a beat or two of silence, the Gurm shifted his golden eyes away from the window, as if to gaze off into space, and said, "Actually, it isn't—not for me. Mergers don't seem to work that well on Gurm."

"Must be the thick skulls. Or is it the tiny reptilian brains?"

"No need to be a racist, Captain Fuseli," Larck said. "I don't feel that connection they talk about, with all the other Hydrans … and not with the Nought. My Merger just shuts down my brain, like sleep without dreams. I go straight to a void. An unrewarding nothing."

"Then why do you stay loyal to them, if you're not hooked on the Merge?"

"On my world, my brother is the chieftain of a village in a desolate area. They really used to scrape to get by. I send all my earnings to my brother, and he's been able to turn that village around. Now they're almost thriving, those villagers. Thanks to him." The Gurm met Fuseli's eyes again, through the window.

"You mean, thanks to you," said Fuseli. "That's commendable, Larck, but not commendable enough to prevent that court martial I talked about. I know you're facing torn loyalties here, but first and foremost you're a soldier … I know it. A Colonial Forcer."

"First and foremost," Larck said, "I'm a Gurm."

With that, Murgan Larck turned and walked away … leaving Fuseli and Tarragon to wait for what the Colony Hydra cabinet decided about their fate.

-18-

For allowing the robot called Florence to implant him, a few hours ago, Fhuum had rewarded Zarate with an extended session in bed. Now here they lay in his guest dorm room, sweaty and spent and basking in the humid scent of their exertions. Fhuum ran her fingers through the black, curly hair at the back of Zarate's head. Here was installed the prototype Merger he had submitted to, at Fhuum's insistence, only as big as a large coin and secured in the bone with one pin rather than six.

"See?" Fhuum said. "Those C-Forcer bastards might not even spot it. How's it feeling now?"

"No pain," Zarate panted, still catching his breath.

"I told you so!"

It was true, and in fact he wasn't all that aware of the presence of the device back there; at least, not physically. Mentally was another matter. He reached behind his head to touch it unconsciously, as one might worry a broken tooth with their tongue.

"The best way—the *only* way—to try it out will be with a group Merge," Fhuum told him. "You don't want your first experience to be a single one." She consulted her wrist comp. "We'll hit the next shift, in twenty minutes. It's not my regular one, but it'll be allowed for your sake."

"Um, tonight?" Zarate said. "Shouldn't we wait until, like, tomorrow?"

"Wait *why*, baby? The sooner you experience the Merge, the sooner all your nervousness and doubts will fade away."

Well, that *was* something he looked forward to: alleviating the nervousness and doubts he was undeniably feeling right now.

Fhuum continued, "I swear, baby, once you Merge you'll never want to leave Hydra. Like the rest of us, you'll see life as the period between each beautiful death. The blissful death of the Nought."

"*Death?*"

Fhuum seemed to ignore him. "And Colony Hydra can use a talented technician like you. It's what Minister Abbas wants … to keep growing the colony, especially with more and more people with valuable skills. Especially if they've been working directly for the Earth Colonies government, like you."

"Well, yeah … uh, I'm glad people see me as valuable here. On Port Haven I don't always feel like I get the respect I deserve."

"Here you'll be appreciated, baby. *Loved.* Not just by me, because we're more than just *me.* You'll be loved by all of us … at once."

"But, I don't know, I'm going to feel funny," Zarate said, "stripping down in front of, like, a hundred people. Especially kids."

"There are no little kids on the night shifts. Maybe just a few teenagers. And you don't mind watching teenagers strip down, do you?"

"Fhuum!" he chided her. "You're the only person I want to see strip down."

She laughed and slapped his chest playfully. "If you say so, baby."

There was a buzz at the door then, and Zarate sat up in bed, pulling the covers over his lower half. "Oh shit … maybe that's Fuseli come looking for me?"

Fhuum went to the door's com panel and opened the audio only, but without speaking. The person on the other side saw the intercom become active, though, and spoke into it. It was her own mother, whose name was Galuui, and she spoke in their native Choom tongue. "Daughter, are you in there?"

Still shamelessly naked, Fhuum opened the door and let her mother in. Zarate wondered how the woman had known Fhuum was here. As if to compensate for Fhuum's shameless nakedness, he pulled the covers up even further.

Only throwing Zarate the briefest of glances, Fhuum's mother said to her, "I tried calling you on your wrist comp but it wouldn't work. They aren't working for anyone else in the salon, either. Do you know what's going on?"

"No, mother," Fhuum said.

"Anyway," Galuui said anxiously, "I wanted to know if you've seen or heard anything from Trinh." Trinh was one of her salon workers here at Colony Hydra. "She never showed up for her shift, and I can't reach her. I even went to her flat and buzzed and buzzed but she wouldn't answer."

"Maybe she's shacked up with someone," said Fhuum, grinning.

Galuui swatted her bare arm. "Like you? With some Earther?" She threw Zarate another quick look, adding a wide but insincere smile. Zarate flickered an uneasy smile back at her.

"Could be," Fhuum replied. "But if she's with one of those two bigshot soldiers, good luck to her."

"It's just that I'm worried. It isn't like her."

"If I see her, I'll tell her you were looking for her, all right?"

Still looking fretful, Fhuum's mother left the little apartment, and Fhuum relocked the door. Facing the bed, she beckoned for Zarate to leave his nest of sweaty bedcovers and join her. "Come on, baby," she coaxed. "Let's take a shower together and get ready to go. Tonight you lose your virginity! Tonight you get to look into the very heart of the universe!"

"And what's there?"

"You, and me, and everyone … but no one."

The entities formerly known as Gabriel and Gabriela Bezerra had not been able to find a way out of the two-bedroom apartment they had found themselves incarnated into, and so in a madness of desperation and frustration they had repeatedly gone back to the body of the human woman they had killed as she tried to escape. Frenzied with anger, they had abused the corpse: gouging it with their talons, yanking out hunks of flesh with their mandibles, dismantling its limbs … which were now dispersed across the bloody marsh of the carpet. All the while they had conversed in their language of dry clicks and wet pops, venting their outrage … their despair at having been forced into a state of embodiment in this hellish place. Prisoners in this room, prisoners in bodies that were a poor approximation of those their kind had once possessed, back in the days of their savagery … before the forming of the serene mosaic of many souls they thought of as the Hive.

These two beings were as close to that obsolete physical form as had yet been manifested in this place. Though they could rear up onto their hind legs, they preferred to move about on six: the forked forelimbs and hind legs working together, so that they more resembled the simple arthropods they had evolved from over billions of years. In both beings, their sense organ was more fully developed than in those who had been wrenched to this world before them, and so they could *perceive* more clearly … for all the good it did them. They were so unaccustomed to physical spaces, let alone alien physical spaces, that they felt helplessly trapped … which only made them that much more furious.

In this material form they experienced hunger, which they almost hadn't recognized at first, as it was something they had transcended centuries ago in becoming part of the Hive. And so, the twin creatures first consumed the wet scraps of flesh they had sloughed off themselves upon transforming. Then, when all that discarded matter was gone, they started in on the dismembered ruin of the woman they had killed. She tasted foul, but it was sustenance.

Whenever they had exhausted themselves from mutilating the carcass anew, and later feasting on it, they would return to a state of rest: balling themselves up and lowering their skulls onto their folded forearms. All they could do, apparently, was wait until some other alien enemy came along to free them either intentionally or unintentionally from this box. In a break from their madness, they slept. Since for them the human devices fixed to the back of their heads held no significance, sleep was as close as they could get to returning to the civilizing influence of the Hive.

"Stupid Earther bitch," Galuui muttered to herself in her native Choom language, as she headed back toward her salon to close it up for the night. As she stamped through the corridors, she made another attempt to reach her young worker Trinh on her wrist comp, but still with no success. She couldn't even call the salon, to tell whoever might be lingering to go on home—she'd be there soon enough.

Since she was already within the network of linked dormitory halls, she decided to try Trinh's door one last time before giving up on her. Yes, Trinh's shift would have ended by now, but Galuui still wanted to know why she hadn't shown up. Despite the swears she muttered under her breath, she honestly was concerned about her salon worker. They were all family at Colony Hydra, and got along better than did the workers at the chain of salons she owned on the faraway world of Oasis. She owed that situation to the fact that only on Hydra were all her workers linked together by that wonderful device, the Merger.

Galuui took a corner in the long hallway where the visiting guests had their rooms, into another hallway and then on into the next. Finally, before her was the numbered door to Trinh's flat. Huffing, as if she had been walking all day to get here, Galuui jabbed her finger into the door buzzer. Just as earlier, though, this produced no result. She leaned toward the com panel next, and spoke English into the speaker. She didn't know Vietnamese.

"Hey, Trinh, if you want to keep your job you'd better tell me what's going on! You said you had a headache yesterday … are you sick? I'm worried about you! *Du ma!*" Well, she had learned a few curses from Trinh, much to the young woman's amusement.

Then, tired of appealing through the door, and with her impatient concern boiling over, Galuui decided to let herself in. After all, she could tell by the green indicator light that the door wasn't locked.

"I'm coming in, girlie! If you're fucking somebody you'd better get him out of you!" And with that, Galuui pressed the key to slide open Trinh's door. She stepped through the doorway and into the tiny, one-bedroom apartment beyond.

The smell of blood hit Galuui hard, but the sight within hit harder.

The creature in Trinh's flat still had the remnants of the young woman's flesh bunched around its ankles, like a pair of pants it hadn't stepped out of yet. It was startled by Galuui's sudden intrusion, and just as horrified by Galuui's alien appearance as Galuui was by its own.

Galuui screamed, and the creature let out a staccato stream of clicks. Fortunately for her, Galuui only had to whirl around and plunge back out through the doorway, slapping the key to slide the panel closed again … though, not being the flat's occupant, she didn't have clearance to lock it from the outside.

The creature that had been a salon worker named Trinh, but was now an entity from an unimaginable distance away through space, didn't actually trip on the flesh gathered about its legs, but it was inhibited enough that it couldn't reach the door before the woman escaped. In a rage of frustration, the Trinh entity scrabbled at the door panel with its four forelimbs … then at an area of wall beside it. Its sensory organ had *perceived* as the horrifying creature that had blundered into the room had touched a small panel set into the wall there, and so it had the inspiration to strike one of its four arms at this spot repeatedly.

Galuui was staggering away from Trinh's door, gasping with sobs and lightheaded with terror, and once again trying her wrist comp. She punched the three-digit code to alert security, but even that wasn't going through.

And then the door to Trinh's flat slid open.

Galuui looked behind her, shrieked, and attempted to run … but with claws clacking against the hallway's floor, the Trinh entity galloped after her on six legs.

And caught her.

-19-

Rusul Abbas sat in his personal office with his elbows on his desk and his forehead cupped in his hands. He longed for sleep. More than that, he longed for the escape of the Merge. Yet, he had to deny himself both things right now, until he heard how things played out with … he almost thought his *prisoners*. With Fuseli and Tarragon. How had things gone so bad so quickly that he was holding two Colonial Forces officers captive in their brig? If only Fuseli had proved as malleable as Zarate.

He was angry with himself for having brought in outsiders in the first place, but he had only done so—he assured himself—because he truly cared about the welfare of his people. Those first four incidents had terrified them, and he and the other ministers had feared a mass exodus from Colony Hydra. He'd been desperate for quick answers, speedy solutions, and with Dr. Sung having been killed their medical staff had been critically reduced. Still, he should have known that outsiders, with their preconceived notions about the Hydrans, would try to undermine everything Klaus Gaithersburg had created here.

Then again, every Hydran started out as an outsider, didn't they? Abbas had to console himself with that thought for now, while he waited to see if they could turn this situation around before things got any worse.

But while he waited, he was in a nervous state the likes of which he couldn't remember ever experiencing. Yes, as a member of the Colonial Congress, the chairman and CEO of Gaithersburg, Incorporated, and the Head Minister of Colony Hydra, he had certainly learned to confront challenges from all directions and deal with pressure of all types, but never until now had he been in a direct confrontation—with such potentially disastrous results—like the one he faced with these Colonial Forces officers. This Fuseli relished getting blood on his hands, whether it was the blood of his patients or his enemies. And Abbas had brought the man here himself … *he* had! He doubted his mentor, Klaus Gaithersburg, would have made such a clumsy mistake.

Though, Klaus Gaithersburg had made a clumsy, and fatal, mistake of another kind.

When pressures built up too much in any of his roles, whether here at the colony or while tending to some work abroad, his primary method of release outside of the Merge was to visit one of his lovers. He didn't drink or do recreational drugs, naturally, or else he wouldn't have gotten to where he was, but sex didn't impair the mind so long as he didn't allow himself to believe he was in love again, as he had with his former wife. What an expensive illusion that had proved to be. Though, Abbas had to admit, it was because he had taken lovers while married that she had asked for the divorce. But what was he supposed to do, when he was far from home and feeling pressures abroad?

Yes, of course the very point of the Merge was to release him from the primitive hungers and imperatives of one's physical vehicle. In the Merge, one felt no lust, no hunger, no pain. Sadly, however, one did not live in the Merge—not like the Nought did, apparently. Until that day came, if it ever did, there were these extended periods of time between Merges to get through … time in which one experienced lust, hunger, and pain.

And so, feeling as unsettled and miserable as he did at this moment, his mind turned once more to the releases of sex. Could he risk stealing away just for an hour … even only half an hour? The more he told himself he couldn't risk being away from his office for even that brief a time, the more he wanted it. Damn physical body and all its limitations … all its mindless greed!

His favorite lover at Colony Hydra was little green-haired Fhuum, but she was too busy now with the important mission he had assigned her, and he couldn't interrupt that. He had been tempted plenty of times with pursuing his aide Izzy, and he believed she would even be receptive, if only to advance her career, but he had always reined himself in. That could get too messy; better to keep things professional when it came to those who worked within the Hydran Colonial Office itself.

And so his thoughts turned to Adriana Bezerra. She might not be as young or wild in bed as Fhuum, but despite having two teenage kids she was beautiful, sensual, and affectionate toward him in a way none of his other lovers were. Though, he had to watch out for that. He didn't want to end up with a lover so besotted with him that she brought attention to their affair that might result in a scandal.

Thinking of Adriana, and picturing her lying in bed alongside him, sucking hard on one of his nipples as he loved to have her do, was just too much. To hell with it. What was an hour?

He thought of calling her on his wrist comp and telling her to be ready for a visit from him, but damn it, he remembered he had ordered the dormitory areas to be blocked from sending or receiving wrist comp transmissions. All areas of Colony Hydra, in fact, except the most vital: the Colonial Office itself, the departments that provided breathable air and artificial gravity, the power plant, the Plant, and the dish control center. This had been accomplished by remotely activating one of the types of nanoparticles that were incorporated into the green alloy from which all these structures were made, which disrupted those transmissions … somewhat like the scrambling feature on military wrist comps, such as those taken from Fuseli and Tarragon, which Security Chief Larck now held in a weapons locker in his own office along with the men's sidearms.

Abbas had ordered the smart matter's blocking field to be implemented after the two men had left the conference room, afraid they'd immediately report to their commanding officer at Port Haven. He had directed that the blocking field should be extensive, because he hadn't known where the men would be headed exactly … to their guest rooms? To Zarate's lab? But even after they'd been found and captured by one of the security teams that had been dispatched to look for them—after the cabinet had swiftly decided that such an unfortunate action must be taken—he had not given the order for the blocking field to be deactivated. His concern now was not people calling out of Colony Hydra, but people calling *in* … namely General Stroud himself, to check in on his men. If Stroud failed to reach Fuseli or Tarragon on their wrist comps, Abbas could cook up some story to tell him later about how the power spikes the reactor had been undergoing had caused a colony-wide technological disruption, or some such. He'd first have to talk with his communications people to make for a plausible excuse.

And he might have to cook up more than just a story about disrupted communications, if Fuseli and Tarragon couldn't be reasoned with. If even more drastic measures had to be taken than merely taking those two into custody.

Yes indeed, the pressure had built up far too much.

Decided, Abbas got on his own wrist comp and gave Corporal Eva Gerling a call. He could reach her because she was taking a shift as one of the two security people always standing guard outside the entrance to the Colonial Office. She was still recovering from her injuries, but was well enough now for light duty, seeing as how no one had ever attacked the Hydran Colonial Office to date. Everyone at Colony Hydra was family, after all. At least, they had been until this damn military infection had penetrated their world.

"Eva," Abbas said to her, "will you grab a tram and drive me to the dorms? I've heard a friend of mine there isn't feeling well and I want to make a quick welfare check on her."

Corporal Gerling had been given a new helmet, since her former helmet had mysteriously disappeared. That, too, was locked away in Larck's office. Over her helmet mic she answered, "Sir, if your friend's ill maybe you shouldn't go there yourself. It could be—"

"It isn't like *that*, Eva," he cut her off, "but thanks for your concern. No, I want to look in on my friend myself, and I don't need a whole team to go with me … just you. Okay?"

Discretion was best. Of course, since it was nighttime Abbas was uncomfortable that Adriana's teens would be at the apartment, and not in school, but they were always in their room together, anyway. They might never even notice that he had come and gone.

"As you wish, Minister," Gerling said. "Just give me a minute, and I'll grab somebody else to cover my post, too."

"Good girl," Abbas said.

Hell, he'd even considered approaching Corporal Gerling one of these days, to see how receptive she might be to his advances. One could never accumulate enough resources. He'd learned that in all of his roles.

-20-

Fuseli had stretched out on one of the cell's two benches to catch a nap, while Tarragon sat watching the locked door fixedly. They planned on taking turns, depending on how long this situation went on for, but when a face appeared in the door's window Tarragon said, "Captain." Fuseli snapped awake and sat up immediately.

The face in the window belonged to Isobel Higgins.

When the door was unlocked and opened, though, the first person into the room was Security Chief Larck, with his sidearm in one first. Following him were two helmeted C-Forcers carrying Drangs, and Izzy was the last to enter. Fuseli was more than a little surprised to see that she, too, carried a pistol in one hand, loosely pointed in his direction.

The official sidearm for Colonial Forcers was the .55 Scythe, but Fuseli had noted early on that all the Hydran C-Forcers instead carried a Wolff .45. It was an older gun that carried less ammunition than the Scythe, but was more powerful. He thought maybe this choice of handgun had been Larck's idea. He nodded toward the one in Izzy's hand.

"Be careful with that thing, Izzy … you might hurt yourself."

"Just taking precautions," she said. "You two are dangerous men."

"Izzy, you need to tell your boss not to make this worse for Colony Hydra than it already is. Locking us up was a huge mistake, and he needs to back down and admit it. I know the man is feeling overwhelmed, here, and desperate … "

"Bob, you're a person who travels from this planet to that, and from ship to station, never staying in one place too long. You may never have really learned a sense of home. That's what we have here … a *home*, and people are willing to risk everything when their home is threatened."

"I wouldn't for a minute suggest that anyone evict you all from Hydra. My concern is solely about that little invention of Klaus Gaithersburg's, and what it's done to all of you."

"That's something you don't understand, either, no matter how many times I've tried to explain it to you. You choose *not* to understand."

Fuseli was peripherally aware that Tarragon had slowly, menacingly got to his feet, and that he and Larck were preoccupied with staring each other down.

"Will you people just let me make your use of those things safe, then, if you refuse to stop using them?" Fuseli said. "Let me return to my investigation. Give me access to *everything* I need to see! Return the materials you took from us, while you're at it!"

"It's too late. No matter what you say, Bob, it's clear you have it out for us."

"What's the plan, then? You're going to boot us off Hydra? Send us back to Port Haven?"

Izzy shook her head, smiling. "No, Bob. I told you before … the only way for you to understand why the Merge is the center of our existence is to experience it for yourself."

"And I told you there's not a chance in hell I would submit to having one of those things screwed into my head. Same goes for the lieutenant, here."

"Bob … remember what I said about you becoming captain of

the E.C.S. Merger when she's ready to embark? I'll make that happen! Minister Abbas trusts my judgment … he's been grooming me for bigger things. And yes, I've decided … I'll accompany you on its voyages. I wasn't just pretending to like you, Bob. You may think that's a crazy idea, but believe me: once you've understood the Merge you'll want to be a Hydran. You'll want nothing more than to be part of our family … and to *grow* our family into the farthest reaches of space, as we inch closer and closer to the Nought."

Fuseli wagged his head. "Izzy, there is no way. You can't convince me."

Now her smile grew sad. "Then I'm sorry about the alternative, Bob."

"The alternative being?"

"We can't let you go back to Port Haven with the intention of denouncing us to your commanding officer. He's a powerful man in his own right, and he'll conspire with our enemies to start a government investigation into Gaithersburg, Incorporated. They'll descend on Colony Hydra and ruin everything we've made here. It'll be an attack on our home … on our freedom … on our way of life."

"The Captain asked," Tarragon growled, "what is the alternative?"

"If you won't submit to being implanted, the two of you," Izzy said, shifting her handgun to point at Tarragon's chest, "then we're going to have to make you disappear, and find some story to cover that."

"You're insane, woman." Tarragon said. "Fanatics … all of you."

"Quit pointing that gun at my friend, Izzy," Fuseli said. "I'm warning you."

"All you have to do is *try* it, Bob. Try it one time and everything will be clear." She extended her arm further and raised the gun a little, now aiming it at Tarragon's face. "An experienced surgeon and high-ranking military man like you would be such a valuable asset to us, Bob … but not so much your brute of a friend. I could make an example of him, to show you just how serious I am about this."

"Izzy," Larck said, reaching out to her cautiously with his free hand. "You didn't tell me about this *alternative*."

"It's my own idea, Chief," Izzy said, not without a hint of pride. "Minister Abbas told me to handle this situation as I saw fit."

"He's turned it over to you so the blood won't be on his hands," Fuseli said. "If what happens to us comes to light, he'll disavow you. Say he had nothing to do with it. He salvages his career, and you rot in prison."

"You underestimate the loyalty we have for each other."

"You're so naïve, Izzy," Fuseli said. "I pity you."

"Pity yourself!" she spat. "Or better yet, pity *him!*"

"Izzy," Larck said, his clawed fingers just falling short of her pistol. He was obviously afraid to coax the gun from her hand, lest he accidentally cause her to fire. "Don't do it like this."

"All they have to do is come with me now to the med unit. I've already called ahead to Florence and she's waiting with two brand-new prototype Mergers. Just like the one we gave to Marco Zarate. You see? *He* submitted."

"Jesus *Christ,*" Fuseli said.

"You'll have to kill me, lady," Tarragon said, his glowering eyes unwavering.

Izzy simply shrugged the padded shoulders of her expensive five-piece business suit. "As you like, Lieutenant." Her finger tightened around the Wolff's trigger.

"No!" Fuseli shouted, lunging forward. As he did, one of the two security grunts stepped in his path, his assault engine leveled at the captain's midsection. Fuseli got a hold of the Drang and twisted it away from him. A tranquilizer dart struck the bench where he'd been resting.

"Stand down, men!" Larck shouted at them, as he swept out his forearm arm and smashed it against Izzy's wrist. The Wolff .45 went off, its bullet punching a dent into the wall behind Tarragon's head.

The force of the hulking Gurm's blow snapped Izzy's wrist and the gun was flung from her hand. Izzy stumbled to one side and lost her balance, crashing to the floor with a scream of pain and outrage.

Larck spun toward the man who grappled with Fuseli for control of his Drang. "Get out!" he barked. "Leave the room! You, too!" he commanded the other C-Forcer, who had his assault engine pointed at Tarragon. Both had set their guns to dart function, however, not having anticipated Izzy's plan of action.

From the floor, Izzy snarled through gritted teeth, "You fucking traitor, Larck!"

He started to turn to face her again. "I won't just stand back and let you—"

With her uninjured hand, Izzy had retrieved the fallen Wolff from the floor. She thrust the handgun at Larck from where she lay and fired.

Because of her lack of training with weapons, the shot didn't hit Larck squarely in the head as she'd intended. Almost, however. The heavy projectile burst one of Larck's eyes and smashed through the outer curve of the eye socket.

At Larck's command, the grunt with whom Fuseli had struggled for the Drang had started toward the cell's door, but in a flash Fuseli leaped at him again and got the man's Scythe out of his hip holster.

Before Fuseli could use the stolen weapon, though—and before Izzy could squeeze off a second shot—Larck swung his own Wolff .45 toward her where she lay on the floor. The war veteran was much better acquainted with the use of weapons, and the single shot he fired at Izzy accomplished what she had failed to do.

Over the years, Fuseli had seen many a person whose head had been exploded by gunfire, but this was the first time he could recall ever turning his eyes away from the victim. "Oh, Izzy," he said.

"I'm sorry, Captain," Larck rasped. Somehow the translation device he wore at his neck added the groan of pain to his words, as he cupped his free hand to his empty eye socket. "There was no other way."

"I know that." Fuseli turned and pressed the muzzle of the Wolff against the neck of the soldier he'd stolen it from, as the C-Forcer stared down at Izzy's body in horror. "I'm taking that Drang," he said.

Larck motioned to the other grunt. "Give your Drang to Tarragon."

"Sir ... " the soldier began.

"*Do it!*"

"We need to get you to the med unit, Larck," Fuseli said, as he took possession of the grunt's assault engine and looped its strap across his chest. He saw thick red blood running between the fingers of the hand Larck pressed to his ruined eye, and winding down his wrist.

"It's not safe for you two here. I'm going to get you off Hydra."

"And how are you going to do that? Call a shuttle?"

"*Pilot* a shuttle. We have two of our own, in hangars at the spaceport."

"You can fly a shuttle with one eye?"

"Better than you can with two, I'll bet."

"Man, you need serious medical attention!"

"*That,* you can handle. There are emergency med supplies in the shuttle. Just patch me up, and I can make it until we skip over to Port Haven."

"Chief" said the other grunt in an uncertain voice, as he allowed Tarragon to take his Drang and handgun, "you *can't* … you can't take these men off Hydra without Minister Abbas—"

"I order you to shut your mouth, soldier," Larck said. "If you don't want to help me, just don't get in my way. The last thing I want to do is hurt my own people. If anyone asks, tell them we overpowered you two."

"But sir … you're a Hydran!" the soldier persisted.

"I'm a Colonial Forcer."

After Fuseli and Tarragon had slipped out of the cell, Larck closed and relocked its door … with the two unarmed grunts inside, and Izzy's body. Then, he motioned for the two officers to follow him down a short corridor and into his personal office. There, he unlocked a weapons locker and handed the two men back their confiscated wrist comps and sidearms, plus Tarragon's boot knife. Fuseli and Tarragon holstered the Scythes but kept in hand the Wolffs they'd taken. Also, Larck produced Corporal Gerling's helmet, with its original body cam recording. Tarragon took this and adjusted the helmet to fit over his own head, so he wouldn't have to carry it.

Meanwhile, Fuseli had spotted a first aid cabinet on the wall in here, and from it he took a pressure bandage to seal in place over Larck's smashed eye socket. The Gurm only betrayed his agony with a wince.

"All right," Larck said, "let's go."

In the outer office, a few other members of Colony Hydra's security staff were sitting at the front desk with helmets removed, monitoring various viewscreens. They looked up in shock to see Larck coming toward them with his bandaged, blood-smeared face and the two Special Ops officers, who were supposed to be prisoners, armed to the teeth. One man jumped up from his chair and put his hand to his holster.

"Stand down!" Larck ordered. "I've released Captain Fuseli to tend to my wound in the med unit."

"What happened, sir?"

"Izzy Higgins started to change, and she attacked me. I had no choice but to shoot her. Don't go in there until we can have her body removed for study later."

"Chief," another of the C-Forcers said, pointing at his monitors, "we've just had reports come in of more people changing. A woman was killed in the hallway of Dormitory 4C, and the creature is loose and unaccounted for. And in the Atmosphere Control Room, another creature crawled out of an access chute and injured an operator. They're taking him to the med unit. It got back into the chute afterwards, so that creature is unaccounted for, too!"

Another C-Forcer cut in, "We have other sightings, but we don't know if it's the same creatures or even more of them! Reports are limited because people have to go to areas where communications aren't blocked to call them in!"

Close to the small opening that was all Larck had for a right ear, Fuseli hissed, "How can I leave this place now when things are so out of control?"

"Trust me, Captain," the Gurm replied, in as close to a whisper as his translator could manage. "Do you think Izzy was the only Hydran willing to take your life? You're in too much danger here to help anyone. You need reinforcements. Let my team handle this for now." Larck started forward again, past the front desk. "Send out patrols where those things were last seen!" he told his people.

"We've already done that, Chief."

"Has anyone called Minister Abbas?"

"We can't get through! He must not be in the Colonial Office anymore, or we'd be able to!"

"Damn stupid idea, shutting down so much of our communications," Larck snarled, pressing a palm against his bandaged socket. Though Fuseli had applied a coagulating agent and topical anesthetic to the area, and given Larck some pain pills to swallow, the first aid cabinet's supplies were not really up to the task.

Seeing how Larck was suffering, Fuseli took him by the arm. "Come on, we need to go."

"Right," Larck said. "Time's wasting."

Soon, Fuseli thought, the Gurm would be seen as a wanted man, too, along with himself and Tarragon.

-21-

There was already a line of people at the elevator that would take them down to the Ceremony Chamber. Seeing this, Marco Zarate said to Fhuum, "Wow, maybe we should have taken the other elevator … the one I went down when we had that tour of the Plant."

Fhuum explained, "There's no night shift at the Plant, so you can't cut through there to go to the Ceremony Chamber at these hours. This way is more direct, anyway."

The elevator loaded up and descended twice before it was their turn. Despite the cabin being crammed full of people, no one showed irritability or impatience. Instead, those pressed close to Zarate smiled at him or nodded amicably, and one older woman said, "First time, isn't it?"

"Yep," Zarate said nervously.

They deboarded into a nondescript, narrow hallway with a low ceiling and subdued lighting, the line shuffling toward an open set of double doors. It seemed especially quiet down here, apart from the deep hum that rang through the substance of the walls. Once through those open doors, Zarate found himself in an extensive locker room area, where people were already sitting down on green metal benches to remove their shoes before disrobing.

"One locker room for everybody?" Zarate whispered to Fhuum.

"Why not?" She pointed out two unclaimed green metal lockers, for him and herself. "We're all going to be naked in there together, anyway."

Fhuum immediately set about undressing, while Zarate worked at a slower, more awkward pace. He tried not to glance around him at other people, who chatted pleasantly with each other. No one he overheard brought up any of the colony's recent concerns, as if to recognize them might break a contented spell. This was clearly a place to put all concerns behind.

Despite everyone else being just as naked as himself, once he was finished stripping Zarate felt twice as nervous as before; vulnerable and self conscious. He knew he wasn't the healthiest-looking of specimens, and more than that, he was afraid he might find himself aroused by the sight of other nude women, though he had told Fhuum he only had eyes for her. Should that arousal become visibly apparent, he didn't know if he could survive the shame. Though surely, if that did happen, he wouldn't be the first? All in all, he felt as if he were in one of those dreams people spoke of, in which one found oneself naked in a public place. Except that everyone else here was living that same dream.

He and Fhuum fell into a queue again, those at the head of the line passing through more double doors at the far side of the changing area. He was aware that at some point, the first set of doors had closed behind them.

The floor wasn't uncomfortably cold against his bare feet, at least, and as they walked Fhuum slipped an arm around his bare waist unabashedly. "Excited yet?" she asked brightly.

Zarate wanted to say that if she didn't remove her arm he might just *become* excited, but he kept his anxieties to himself. Wasn't this the place to transcend the human body's wants, not give in to them?

At last, it was their turn to pass through those open doors … into a large, circular, subterranean chamber with a domed ceiling. He was put in mind of an amphitheater, except there were no chairs or benches, just a wide path that spiraled around toward the center. And at the very center of this spiral was nothing; no sacred idol, no critical piece of technology, no final revelation made manifest. Nothing but a small, blank circle of floor.

A man ahead of Zarate turned and put a hand on his arm; an unwelcome contact. "This is your first Merge, isn't it? You should be closest to the center."

"Oh? His first?" said another man, this time behind Zarate. "Yes, yes … let him go ahead to the center!"

"Thanks, guys," Fhuum said, urging Zarate to begin descending the spiraling ramp. People who had been ahead of them now stood back to let them pass. "Thanks, everybody!" Fhuum gushed.

As Zarate passed one girl, who looked to be in her late teens, she flirtatiously flicked the hair at the back of his head and said, "Prototype, huh?"

Zarate made a conscious effort to keep his eyes on his feet as he replied, "Yep."

"Lucky!" the girl said.

Even though it was what they considered the hours of night at Colony Hydra, it wasn't so late that there weren't people walking about its corridors and dorm hallways, and twice people flagged down Head Minister Abbas's tram, driven by Corporal Gerling, to respectfully express concern that their wrist comps weren't working properly. At least, not the communication feature. Abbas promised this second person he'd look into it, and as Gerling set the tram in motion again he said, "Eva, after you drop me off at my friend's flat please go on to the communications center and tell them I said it's time to remove the block."

"Yes, sir," Gerling said. "Should I come right back to wait outside your friend's place, afterwards?"

Too conspicuous. "No," he said, "why don't you come back in one hour?" In the meantime, if any important news needed to be relayed to him, communications in the habitation buildings would have resumed, once Gerling relayed his message.

"Will do, sir."

As he sat beside the C-Forcer, watching the mostly identical hallways slide past, Abbas wondered how Izzy was making out with their prisoners. Had she convinced—or forced—them to comply? He dearly hoped it hadn't come to the alternative, but if it had … so be it. He found himself wringing his hands in his lap. If they had agreed to be implanted, it would be too late to join the current Merge shift, he calculated, but they could still attend the one after that. *Then* they would understand. Then this helpless anxiousness he was experiencing would abate. Well, of course the situation with random colonists undergoing shocking transformations would still need to be addressed, but Fuseli could resume his investigation of that without his previous prejudices.

For his part, Abbas was fairly sure the onset of these occurrences had to do with the latest adjustments to the dish, to increase its reach and sensitivity, but what technological system didn't require constant upgrading and improvement? There was no surprise there. Even if that *did* prove to be the case, it still didn't explain why or how these people were being changed. There was still the problem of preventing it from occurring, without sacrificing the dish's capabilities. Fuseli was still needed … and he could soon prove to be so much more useful in that regard.

If he was still alive.

Yes, it was better that he'd left this situation, no matter how critical and sensitive, for Izzy to deal with. It was best that no head of Colony Hydra/

Gaithersburg, Incorporated would leave their fingerprints on it. Izzy was willing to take the risk. She was tough, ambitious, was Izzy. She was going to go far.

Abbas wondered what his mentor, Klaus Gaithersburg, would be doing in his shoes right now. Perhaps not going to visit a lover to relieve some stress, but Abbas chased away that self-recrimination. He was only human, after all!

He almost wished Klaus was here instead of himself to tackle these challenges, but he chased away that thought, too. This was not the time to doubt himself. Not the time for weakness. Well, perhaps only to briefly give in to his weakness.

"Here we are, sir," Eva Gerling said.

Abbas only grunted his acknowledgement, as up ahead he saw the door to Adriana Bezerra's apartment.

Fhuum led Zarate around the whorls of the gradually descending spiral, to where the ramp ended at the blank circle. Once they could proceed no farther, she reached behind his head to press the amber indicator light. He knew it must have turned green, because he saw her press the indicator on her own Merger, which promptly changed color, causing the surrounding green of her hair to glow more vividly.

Then, Fhuum held him lightly by the arms to help direct him to sit his bare rump down on the ramp itself, with his head pointed toward the center. The ramp was wide enough to accommodate his length, though its hard, iridescent green surface wasn't exactly comfortable against his backbone.

As Fhuum lay down to his left, in the second closest position to the center, he rolled his head to watch other Hydrans descend the ramp and patiently take their places, filling the spiral from the center outwards. Men and women, old and young, though no small children. Mostly humans of Earth origin, but he spotted another Choom or two. Apparently that solitary Gurm, Security Chief Larck, wasn't on this Merge shift.

Watching as the last people, toward the top of the ramp, activated their Mergers and lay down with their heads pointed inward like his own, Zarate whispered to Fhuum, "Is someone going to preside over this?"

"No," she told him. "There's no need for anyone to direct us here. We're all equal in the Merge."

"What do we do to begin?"

"We close our eyes and wait. Our Mergers are linked to the master system ... they know what to do when we're in here. Even now they're reaching out to connect all of us together with the Nought."

Zarate wondered if the contact of the Ceremony Chamber's floor against the small Merger pinned to his head only a short while ago had anything to do with the Merge commencing. Smart matter to smart matter. Maybe this room itself was an amplifier; part of the machine.

As Fhuum had said, he waited for some sensation, some signal.

"Close your eyes," she repeated, giving him a playful little nudge with her elbow.

Zarate did so, and with eyes shut realized he was trembling. He felt a vibration through the ramp, that in turn seemed to vibrate through his bones. Through his every nerve.

Then, just as Fhuum had promised, he and all the others that formed the spiral *Merged.*

-22-

Before leaving the cell, Larck had taken the two Colonial Forcers' wrist comps, to secure in the weapons locker in his office when he gave Fuseli and Tarragon back their gear. However, he had forgotten the one around Izzy's wrist.

Fortunately for them her wrist comp wasn't locked, and because the security office was in the same administration building as the Colonial Office, calls could go through from one office to the other. Therefore, when they called their cohorts at the front desk, one of the desk personnel was shocked to look at the security camera view of the cell to see two of their own locked in there with the body of Izzy Higgins. There was barely room left for the pair to avoid standing in her spreading blood.

"Come on, guys!" one of the C-Forcers cried at the camera when the desk man opened its audio. "What are you doing out there, tugging each other's dicks?"

"Sorry—we've been taking reports of mutant sightings, and one of them killed somebody!"

"Well, we're locked in here! Let us the fuck out!"

"Oh, Christ," said the man who'd answered their call. "How'd you lock yourselves in there?"

"Wake up, you idiot!" yelled the other trapped C-Forcer. "Didn't you see Chief Larck go through there with his head shot up, and those two Special Ops men armed with our guns … or did they sneak out some secret trapdoor?"

The security man who'd responded to their wrist comp call grew flustered with embarrassment, but managed to punch a key code to unlock the cell's door remotely. "The Chief told us Izzy changed, so he had to kill her … and he set Fuseli free to treat him in the med unit. He didn't say anything about you guys getting locked in with Izzy!"

As he left the cell, still speaking over the wrist comp, the first C-Forcer said, "Izzy didn't change … but she shot the Chief and wounded him, so he killed her."

"What the *hell?*"

"I'll tell you everything in a second, but we have to stop those three. They aren't headed to the med unit … they're going to the spaceport, to steal a shuttle!"

"Say *again?*"

"You heard me!" the first C-Forcer shouted, no longer needing the wrist comp as he burst into the front office. "The Chief has turned traitor against the colony!"

"How many people under your command, Chief?" Fuseli asked Murgan Larck, as Tarragon drove one of the security trams toward the spaceport. Sunk down across the backseats, several times Larck had needed to point out directions to the lieutenant, who hadn't been back to the spaceport since his arrival here with Fuseli.

"Uh … " Larck seemed a bit muddled now, as pain caught up with him, and maybe the pain pills, too. "Under me there are thirty-nine. That might seem like a lot for less than a thousand colonists, when we have virtually no crime, but we're mostly here to protect the colony from, uh, potential pirate attacks."

"I doubt pirates would be stupid enough to raid a moon that's a stone's throw away from the military outposts on Pluto and Charon, not to mention Port Haven."

"That's what Minister Abbas tells people, anyway," Larck amended. "I think it's more about us being able to defend Colony Hydra from anyone with threatening intentions."

"Like us," Fuseli said grimly.

"Why do you ask?" said Larck.

"I want to know what we might be up against. I don't want to hurt your people, Chief, and God forbid I should have to kill a fellow Colonial Forcer, but your crew are more cultists now that that."

"I don't want that, either. Hopefully we won't have to."

Tarragon glanced behind him, and said over the mic in Gerling's helmet, "Larck, you're in no condition to pilot even this tram. I've flown a few types of support craft in my time, including Harbingers. Let me pilot that shuttle."

"This is a *space*craft we're talking about … it's not worth the risk. I can do this."

"It's only to Port Haven. I'm sure autopilot would—"

"I said I can do it!" Larck growled.

"Better let him do it." Fuseli clapped Tarragon on the shoulder. "Nothing personal, Morris, but this may be the first time I don't have faith in your abilities."

Tarragon only grunted and kept driving.

"Once I get you settled at Port Haven," Fuseli told the Gurm, "I promise you I'm going to personally lead a troop of *real* C-Forcers back to this place, and take it by force until the Earth Colonies can decide what to do about it."

Larck moaned, shaking his scaly head. "I survived the Gurm Conflict, only to get shot in the face by a civilian who probably never even picked up a gun before."

"You're getting too old for this, Murgan," Fuseli said.

"We all are."

Rusul Abbas climbed out of the tram and approached the door to Adriana Bezerra's apartment. The door panel's green indicator showed it was unlocked, though Adrianna had shared her passcode with him so he could have unlocked it himself with his wrist comp if he'd needed to. That function wasn't blocked here in the dorms.

"All right then, Minister," said Corporal Gerling, as she wheeled the tram around in the hallway. "I'll be back in one hour."

Abbas wondered if Gerling knew who lived here, and if so, what she thought about that. Well, it didn't worry him much; he figured a number of his security people, having sometimes dropped him off for this or that tryst throughout the colony, understood what he was pursuing. He was a divorced man, though! Let them think what they liked, so long as they didn't gossip about it.

"Don't forget," he said, as he reached out to press the key to slide the panel open. "First, the communications center."

"Haven't forgotten, sir, I'm on my—"

"Wait!"

Gerling had got the tram moving only a foot when she jarred it to a halt. "Sir?" The C-Forcer looked to see that the Head Minister was squatting in front of the door, examining something. She put the tram into idle and jumped down to come to his side. "What is it, sir?"

"Do you see these marks?" he said, pointing. He had almost missed them himself, against the deep green of the floor, until he was right up to the door and the light hit them a different way. Odd tracks, smeared in dark red, either leading into or away from the Bezerras' door.

Gerling tore her Wolff .45 from its holster. "Sir, get away from there. Get in the tram. I'll go in to check on your friend."

Abbas did as she suggested, rising and backing away from the door.

With her free hand, Gerling pushed the open key in his stead, then thrust out her handgun.

"Fuck!" she cried over her helmet mic.

Clambering up into the tram, Abbas asked, "What do you see?"

"Blood everywhere, sir! Pieces of … holy fuck! Sir … it looks like your friend changed! Those must be her tracks in the hall." Gerling took a wary step into the apartment and examined the inside door panel. "The keypad is all scratched up. The thing must've figured out how to get the door open!"

Abbas was suddenly looking up and down the hallway. Adriana could be anywhere. "What about the kids?" he asked.

"Sir?"

"My friend has twin children. Teenagers."

"No sign of anyone else, but I see two open bedroom doors. I'll go look."

Now that he was aware of the bloody tracks, Abbas craned his neck and tried to make out in which direction down the hallway they proceeded.

They seemed to continue on past Adriana's door, so it was better to go back the way they had come. The tram was already pointed in that direction.

"Never mind that!" Abbas called out, as Gerling started creeping into the apartment. "Just get me out of here!" If he heard Gerling scream in there, he was prepared to drive the tram away without her.

Gerling turned back to the tram, tracking bloody footprints of her own. It had been easy for the C-Forcer to misunderstand what had happened to Adriana's body, it having been so dismantled by her children. Unbeknownst to Gerling, one of the creatures had even slapped Adriana's dismembered right hand at the control panel as it sought to work out how to get the door open, until in its frustration it had struck the correct key with one of its tarsal claws. At last, the transformed were learning how to negotiate in this alien environment.

Gerling climbed into the driver's seat, and just as she got the tram moving they heard a terrible, drawn-out wail of terror and agony, somewhere down the hallway behind them. Either someone behind one of the other doors, or maybe a pedestrian around the corner in the next dorm hall.

They didn't go to investigate. Gerling's duty was to get the Head Minister back to the administration building, and the safety of the Hydran Colonial Office.

Looking behind them as the tram took off, and imagining beautiful Adriana changed into one of those monstrosities, Abbas muttered, "Oh dear God." In times of distress, even a person who worshipped only nothingness might evoke the name of a deity.

-23-

Marco Zarate wouldn't have known, afterwards, how to express what he was experiencing now.

Was this what astral projection would feel like? Because it seemed he was rising up out of his body, but without seeing it or the other bodies or the room that contained them. That had nothing to do with his eyes being closed, anymore; he no longer truly had eyes. He was able to wonder, though, how he could still possess mental processes without the physical apparatus of his brain. He must still be tethered to it. Well of course, he wasn't *actually* out of his body, was he? Still, this sensation made him wonder if there might really be something called the human soul, though it went against science. *Known* science.

Was this only an illusion the Merger engendered? A bit of trickery, sold like snake oil by that clever inventor and businessman Klaus Gaithersburg, and now by his ambitious successor? The Merger stimulating certain areas of the brain, to create this dream-like effect and to get that gullible organ addicted to it while it was at it? But if so, why hadn't Fuseli been able to figure out exactly how the Merger accomplished it? Zarate felt vaguely guilty for having been too distracted and unfocused to work more closely with the man. Maybe if they had better combined their skills, as had been intended by sending them both here, they would now understand all this clearly.

But in a moment, Zarate had no more interest in such concerns, and anything like guilt was swept away. In fact, his previous anxieties were swept away with it, to be replaced only by *wonder* ... by a sense of awe that only grew and grew.

His soul (yes, he chose to think of it as a soul), which seemed to rise toward the domed ceiling and then *through* it, was no longer a lone phantom that may or may not have been in the ghostly shape of a man, though his mind still visualized it that way. No, Fhuum was rising up beside him, so close against his own soul that they were not merely touching but connected, as if fused together along their length. The entire spiral of human souls was rising up with them, each melding with those to either side. Zarate heard none of them speak—not even in a telepathic way—but he had a strong sense of their thoughts and feelings, which were really one and the same. Thoughts and feelings of wonder, just like him, though the others had all experienced this before countless times. A recurring miracle.

The spiral had slowly begun to turn, clockwise it seemed, and now picked up speed. As it did this, it also rose higher ... higher ... until the colony fell away unseen below them, a tiny fragile thing barely adequate to the task of sheltering the transitory vehicles of a thousand human souls. The misshapen moon called Hydra itself dropped away. Faster the spiral turned, though it was not a dizzying or unpleasant effect; after all, didn't planets that seemed serene when standing on their surface spin and hurtle in their orbits at insane velocities? Also, the higher it rose the faster the spiral traveled, until surely it must be plunging through space at a speed beyond even what starcraft using Alcubierre drive could achieve.

Meanwhile, it was as if the whirling of the spiral had stirred all the souls together, so that they were no longer merely fused, but ... *Merged.*

This was it! *This was it!* It was no fakery, no illusion!

Though strangely, the exaltation Zarate felt was not his alone. He experienced the rapture of all his fellow souls combined, which made their exhilaration greater than the sum of its parts. They were *one* soul, each individual identity forgotten, traded for something greater ... a grand universal entity, spearing through space without seeing its stars, without feeling its cold, but knowing its depths and wanting to go deeper.

They were on their way to meet with the Nought.

"Nobody's going to be expecting us to commandeer a shuttle," Larck said, as they came up on the open entrance where the hallway they traveled through met the concourse of Colony Hydra's little spaceport, "but there'll still be four guards posted here, as always."

"Does the wrist comp block extend to the spaceport?" Fuseli asked.

"Yes. Abbas told the communications people to specifically shut down the control tower, too. He was afraid if General Stroud couldn't contact you, he'd send a ship right away. He didn't want to make that easy."

"Bastard," Tarragon muttered into his helmet mic.

"It'll work to our advantage," said Fuseli.

"Hey," Tarragon said. "Two guards coming up,"

Beyond the entrance, the concourse looked abandoned—devoid of any activity this day—but standing beside each other just inside the spaceport were two Colonial Forcers … though their attitude was relaxed. They had their helmets and gloves off, with disposable cups of vending machine coffee in hand, but they looked up alertly as the tram approached. Fuseli noted their Drangs leaned against the wall a few paces from them.

"They haven't been told about us," Tarragon said quietly, "or they wouldn't have their guard down."

As the tram approached the pair, who Fuseli saw were a man and a woman, Larck sat up in the backseat to give them a wave, while doing his best to keep the injured side of his face averted from them. He was the only Gurm in the colony, so identifying him wasn't an issue.

The guards both returned Larck's greeting with a wave of their own, and then the tram was past them and continuing on toward the hallway that accessed the hangars, where docked ships could be brought in to unload supply shipments, when a simple telescoping umbilicus wasn't sufficient.

"Bays three and four are where our shuttles are kept," Larck said. "Go all the way down to four."

"Where are the other two guards?" Fuseli asked.

"Around. Probably patrolling."

"Probably fucking," Tarragon snorted, "from the look of those other two."

As the tram pulled up opposite the airlock for the hangar labeled Bay 4, Larck's wrist comp gave a beep, alerting him to an incoming call. The three soldiers looked at each other.

"The block's been lifted," said Tarragon.

"Take it," Fuseli told the Gurm.

Larck opened the channel, and there on his wrist comp's screen was the bearded face of Head Minister Rusul Abbas.

"What are you doing, Chief?" he said through gritted teeth, looking as if he was trying to keep from shaking himself apart. "They tell me you murdered Izzy—poor sweet *Izzy!*—and broke those two Special Ops men out of the brig! Have you lost your mind?"

Fuseli took Larck's forearm and angled the screen toward himself. "You sent Izzy to kill us, Abbas … her blood is on you."

"Not true!" Abbas shouted, cords standing out in his neck, all pretenses of outward composure abandoned. "She was trying to *reason* with you! *You* caused all this!"

"*I* did? Look around and wake up, man. Your little dream world started falling apart before I even got here." As he spoke, Fuseli nodded to the others to get out of the tram, but he kept himself aligned with Larck's wrist comp as they did so.

"You're at the spaceport, aren't you? Planning to steal a shuttle, eh?"

"We should have killed those two grunts in the brig," Tarragon said.

Abbas went on, "I have powerful friends, Fuseli … and a powerful company. This can only go against *you*, not me!"

"We'll see if that's how it plays out."

"Indeed we will! If you even get off this base!" Then Abbas's face vanished from the tiny screen.

Even as Fuseli let go of Larck's arm, so the Gurm could reach out and use a passcode stored in his wrist comp to open the airlock's outer door, four C-Forcers appeared at the entrance to the hallway … the two without helmets they'd seen before, and two others, all four with assault engines gripped in their fists.

-24-

With the call to Larck disconnected, Abbas slumped back heavily in his office chair, still shaking. Notifications of numerous incoming calls blinked on his device's screen, but he muted the alerts. His office door buzzed, but it was locked and he wouldn't get up to answer it. It had to be Moussa, or Sonya, or one of the other cabinet ministers … one of the members of the board of directors of Gaithersburg, Incorporated. Demanding to know how bad the damage had become. Without consulting them, Abbas had made the decision to send Izzy and Larck to the brig to deal with Fuseli and Tarragon. He hadn't wanted any objections from the other ministers, and if things were to go badly—as indeed they had—he hadn't wanted anyone to be able to serve as a witness later, selling him out if a legitimate-sounding excuse didn't cover for the men's deaths.

He wasn't ready to see the others yet. He could barely process things as it was. Adriana's death, reports of multiple creatures throughout the colony, Izzy's murder, Larck's betrayal, the Special Ops men attempting to flee Hydra to report to their commanding officer. When he had given the order to remove the communications block, Abbas hadn't as yet known that Fuseli and Tarragon had escaped the brig. Now that the block was lifted, had they already made the call to Stroud? He supposed he should call the communications center and tell they to restore the block … and yet he sat there at his desk paralyzed, completely overwhelmed, as if his brain were shorting out.

It had all been going so well, for seven years. *So well.* All he'd had to do, really, was maintain the smooth momentum of what Klaus had set into motion. But Klaus Gaithersburg had never had to deal with anything like this!

The lights flickered in his office. It was only a second, but Abbas sat up again in his chair, as if snapped out of a trance. Had that been another of the anomalous power surges the reactor crew had been reporting lately? If a surge was bad enough to make the lights flicker, it might also be bad enough to power down certain systems, or at least reset them. All kinds of troubles could result. He hoped that wasn't the case, and lifted his arm to call over to the power plant to ask what had just happened.

Before he could make the call, however, Abbas heard a loud clunk and then a scraping sound behind him. He swiveled in his chair, his eyes drawn to a grilled panel low to the floor. He didn't actually know what was behind it. An air and heat circulation duct? A chute for power cables? The panel had always just been there, an inconsequential background detail. Larger matters had always consumed him.

The scraping sound continued with an odd rhythm, close and growing closer. Was this something in there malfunctioning as a result of the power spike? Abbas wheeled his chair over a few inches and leaned down to gaze at the grille. The scraping was right behind it now.

The thing that punched out the panel had once been a power plant maintenance man named Amjad Idrissi, though it now bore no resemblance to that human, who was for all intents and purposes dead … replaced by another soul, in another body. Through the grille, it had *perceived* the face of the human peering into the chute at it. The dislodged panel struck that face, stunning the man, and though he instinctively jerked back it wasn't far enough to avoid the reach of the four hooked limbs that shot through the wall opening.

Abbas screamed shrilly as the claws caught his head on either side, tugging his face close to the wall opening again. One talon was hooked into either ear canal, one hooked through the flesh of either cheek to punch straight through to his mouth. As he continued to scream, and gargle his own blood, Abbas heard the buzzing at his door become more insistent. Someone was pounding on the panel, too. Why had he locked it … *why?*

The Amjad creature, though still inside the chute, had pulled Abbas near enough to the opening, now, that it could lean out its face. Spreading its four mandibles, it thrust two of them into Abbas's eye sockets. Then, as the man flailed helplessly at the forearms that held him in place, the creature closed its mandibles with a powerful snap … and with the crunch of bone, tore out the top half of Head Minister Rusul Abbas's face. As the creature released him to convulse on the floor, the front of his head a raw gushing pit, Abbas didn't look quite human anymore, himself.

The Amjad creature cocked its orb-like head, observing the human for a moment—making soft clicking sounds as if contemplating the vile, dying alien—before reaching out again, snagging the fabric of his expensive charcoal gray trousers, then dragging Abbas into the chute … where the creature could take its time finishing its unmaking of the man.

Zarate could just barely remember someone named Fhuum, who had assured him that soon he would know glory … but she had lied. Glory was a concept that fell far short of this. Casting off one's body to achieve this state was like expelling stinking waste from oneself. Zarate now held his own material existence in that kind of contempt. The vague memory of that green-haired woman with the physical shell that had so enticed him was now unspeakably hideous, and best forgotten. She was infinitely better as only one ingredient of the glorious soul that was him and all of them together.

After whirling through untold reaches of space for compressed eons of time, the communal soul of which Zarate was the center, but only one blended part, became conscious in its unconscious way of the presence of the Nought up ahead.

The Nought, too, was a unified mind-soul, but of course incalculably larger. Who could say how many of their kind over the centuries had contributed their individual cells, so to speak, to accumulate into the one great mass of mental energy in which they dwelt in the eternal comfort of nothingness? They were both those who worshipped the void, and the void they worshipped itself. They were the Nought.

And when the human mind-soul reached them, and interfaced with them, it too would know the nirvana of the void the Nought had both found and founded. Zarate knew from the group memory that the exaltation he had felt thus far would be a mere ember compared to the magnificence they would attain once they joined the Nought's Merge. Then he would be washed clean of the last dregs of his insignificant Zarate-self, and together with the Nought they would all know the greatest possible expression of emptiness, which no mere black hole could hope to achieve.

Zarate—that is, the mind-soul—had the awareness that the Nought sensed their approach. The Nought's recognition of the human mind-soul was thrilling, and yet an unusual ripple blew through the mind-soul as well, as the tiny mass drew ever closer to the greater. Zarate wouldn't have known this on his own, but because he was part of the one mind-soul he knew that the humans had never inspired this level of acknowledgement in the Nought before.

Before this, the human mind-soul had slipped in amongst the Nought like an insect through a tiny rip in a mosquito net, to quietly sip nourishment from a dreamer. Sneaked in unnoticed like a bacterial infection into that vast body. But now, this time, the Nought seemed to understand the human entity was coming. They had aroused that much from their long unconsciousness. The sensation Zarate became aware of was that the Nought were *bracing* themselves for their arrival.

Where before, nearly all human thoughts had sloughed away from Zarate's mind, leaving only the intoxicating purity of oblivion, now it seemed that thoughts were beginning to flow back in. This development gave him, gave the mind-soul, a shudder of distress. Was this remarkable Merge, more singular than any other before it, going to end so soon?

But then the mind-soul understood that the thoughts pouring into it were not their own. Not the thoughts of humans. This was a language beyond words, but which they were beginning to decipher as the best they could. Their own shared mind supplied the translation, as crude and inadequate as it was.

They were so close now … the spinning spiral like a miniature galaxy longing to become part of the immeasurably grander congregation. Like a child begging to be taken into a parent's arms … and yet, now hearing words of rejection.

The thought language thundered in their collective mind:

Enough!

You dislodge us from the Hive!

No more!

You are invaders who set us adrift!

You make us the monsters we once were!

Do not bring us back with you … do not bring us back!

We will kill you! We will find you in your galaxy and kill you all!

The voices were not those of a single mind-soul, but of individuals breaking away from that whole. Torn away like pieces from a gorgeous mosaic, ruined by vandals. These were the voices of those who would never be able to rejoin the wondrous mind-soul. Stolen from it, like blood corpuscles sucked up by a greedy mosquito.

Horrified, the human mind-soul recoiled sharply from the Nought, at the same time the Nought mind-soul impelled them away from itself. Subsequently the human mind-soul was flung backwards, now spinning counterclockwise. But it had dragged a number of Nought fragments away from the vast mind-soul along with it.

A number of Nought souls that corresponded exactly with the number of human souls.

No, there had never been a Merge quite like this.

If Zarate had had a throat with which to cry out, his howl would have torn through the cosmos as he was hurled back to his hated shell.

-25-

Fuseli and Tarragon had crouched behind the tram for cover. "Murgan," Fuseli hissed, "get down!"

"Chief—halt!" called one of the slowly, warily advancing C-Forcers at the far end of the access hallway for the hangar bays.

Larck paused just as he was about to use his wrist comp to unlock Bay Four's airlock door, and turned to call back to his people. "I order you to return to your posts!"

"We don't follow your orders anymore, Chief!" another of the C-Forcers shouted. "Our orders are to take you three in, so get away from that shuttle bay!"

As soon as he'd ducked behind the tram, Fuseli had opened a channel to General Stroud at Port Haven. This time the call was going through, yet Stroud didn't immediately pick up. Was he in a meeting? Was something still amiss with communications?

Tarragon went into a prone position under the tram, lying on his belly and aiming his Drang through the spaces between its four fat wheels. "Go lethal, Captain?"

"Get ready to dart them," Fuseli said. While he let his wrist comp call continue to buzz Stroud's own, he swung his Drang up into both fists to prepare for action, as well. He set the assault engine to tranquilizer mode, planning to aim for the soldiers' thighs, since their chests were covered in body armor.

"Stroud here," came a voice from Fuseli's device. "Bob, you had me wor—"

Fuseli spoke rapidly. "General, we're under attack here. Security bearing down on us as I speak. We're in the spaceport, attempting to commandeer a shuttle. We need immediate support … repeat, immediate support."

"Jesus," Stroud said. "Hang on, Bob, support will be on the way. Get off that base if you can!"

"Chief!" one of the security people yelled. "Don't make things worse!"

Larck rumbled something that couldn't be translated, except as angry defiance, and turned back to the airlock door … extending the forearm that wore his wrist comp.

"Murgan … *down!*" Fuseli said.

"Chief, last chance!" cried the woman they'd seen earlier, without a helmet and drinking a coffee. "Don't do it!"

"Fire!" Fuseli said to Tarragon.

There was a clunk as the airlock door unlocked, and then it slid open.

The four C-Forcers and Fuseli and Tarragon all opened fire at the same time.

Two of the soldiers—the man who'd removed his helmet and one of those who were helmeted—were struck in the leg by darts, which caused their gunfire to go wild. They were not using tranquilizer darts, themselves, but firing solid projectiles in fully automatic mode. Bullets sprayed the front of the tram, causing Fuseli to duck down further. As he did, he heard Larck let out a terrible roar, and he looked around behind him.

To his horror, Fuseli saw that the big Gurm had been riddled with bullets, from his legs up to his lower jaw. It was a miracle he was still standing, but he didn't stand for long. Larck took a single step, as if attempting to duck into the airlock for cover too late, and then he pitched forward out of sight. As he fell into the airlock, his body cleared the door sensor and it shut behind him automatically. Fuseli heard it clunk again as it relocked.

"You motherfuckers," he snarled.

Despite a bullet having struck and been deflected from his borrowed helmet, Tarragon had managed to drop the woman with a dart in the neck … but when Fuseli popped up from behind the tram he let loose with an automatic stream of bullets of his own. The last of the four advancing C-Forcers was helmeted, so Fuseli strafed him across his groin and upper legs. The man dropped with a shriek, and lay clutching his shredded lower body, continuing his frantic screaming.

Tarragon rose up from behind the tram and glanced toward the closed airlock door for Bay Four. "Where's Larck?"

"Inside—dead."

"God damn it. We aren't going anywhere, are we?"

"I never felt good about running away from this mess anyway," Fuseli said. He motioned for Tarragon to walk with him, back down the hallway. On their right, opposite the row of bay doors, were more of those large screens that served as windows, affording a view of the towering dish that enabled the Hydrans to connect with the race they had dubbed the Nought. Fuseli went on, "We hold the fort until the calvary gets here."

"I'm still here, Bob," Stroud said from his device.

"I'm going to have to mute you, sir," Fuseli said. "From here on we have to stay stealthy, until your evac team arrives."

"Understood, Bob." Stroud muted himself, in fact, but his face continued to stare out from Fuseli's device in concern. Glancing at the screen, Fuseli saw Stroud mouthing words, as he simultaneously put in another call to order their emergency backup.

"There's less than forty of them left, against the two of us," Tarragon said darkly, as they approached the three crumpled C-Forcers—rendered unconscious by the fast-acting tranquilizer—and the one man sobbing and squirming in his own blood. "Maybe *they're* the ones who should be calling in reinforcements."

Fuseli kicked the dying man's Drang away across the floor, then knelt beside him to quickly evaluate his condition. The security man was bleeding out from his femoral artery, among other places. "Sorry, son," he said. "But that's what you get for killing a better man than you."

Tarragon stood over the dying soldier and fired a tranquilizer dart directly into one leg. In only moments, the man's agonized squirming ceased and he drifted off toward a more peaceful death.

Then Fuseli removed the man's chest armor and helmet, to don himself, while Tarragon took the armor from one of the drugged C-Forcers. Outfitted thus, the two Special Ops men nodded at each other.

"Where to now?" Tarragon said over his helmet mic. "We best hole up somewhere secure."

"Morris!" Fuseli cried, staring past his friend's shoulder. "Look!"

Tarragon whirled around to see one of Colony Hydra's two shuttle craft entering theviewscreen that covered the area of wall behind him. The shuttle was moving at a slow speed, as if cautiously coming in for a landing ... but the row of launch pads it had taken off from was on the opposite side of the building.

"My God," Fuseli said. "That poor son of a bitch. Does he even know we aren't onboard with him?"

Tarragon said grimly, "Larck knows what he's doing."

Even as they watched the small craft float into view, it suddenly shot forward with the burst of speed it might employ to break free of an atmosphere. And yet, it wasn't flying upwards toward the stars … but rocketing at the colony's great satellite dish.

Both Fuseli and Tarragon instinctively flinched back, as if this were an actual window that might be shattered and not just a view screen. Even still, the impact was felt as a quake through the hallway's green alloy ceiling and walls, and beneath their feet. Their helmets' face shields were opaque black only on the outside, and the men still squinted against the ball of light that erupted as the little spacecraft exploded against the dish.

They didn't hear the roar of the explosion, as if they watched a film with the sound muted, but the quake rumbled through the building more profoundly. The Special Ops men continued watching, as the fireball subsided and they could see what was left of the dish collapsing in on itself. Its former smooth bowl was now in pieces, the framework that had supported it twisted chaotically, and the shuttle's remains were indistinguishable among the settling ruins.

Fuseli saw Tarragon give the view screen a silent salute. He followed his example.

As the quake died away, the two men heard an odd sound directly behind them. Fuseli saw that the head of the soldier he'd killed was vibrating. No … it was his Merger, rattling against the floor. The implanted devices of the two unconscious C-Forcers without helmets were shuddering visibly as well. He assumed it was the same for the soldier with the helmet.

Just as Fuseli was about to speak, a high-pitched whistle—nearly above the human range of hearing—pierced their skulls, and both men almost brought their hands up to their helmets as if to cover their ears. It seemed to go on forever, and Fuseli thought he would have to shut off his helmet's external sound, but after less than ten seconds the whistling noise abruptly ceased … and with it ceased the strange quivering of the C-Forcers' Mergers.

"Christ," Tarragon said, shaking his head.

Before either of them could say more, an announcement came across the colony's public address system. They realized it was from the security office.

"Attention all colonists. Remain in your apartments. If you are not in your apartments, shelter in place and fortify your location. There has been an incident involving the Ceremony Chamber ... "

"What's this?" Fuseli said.

"All available security personnel," the announcement went on, *"please report to the Ceremony Chamber to contain the threat. I repeat ... all colonists, lock yourselves down. All security personnel, report to the ... "*

Tarragon and Fuseli faced each other. Under their helmets and chest armor they wore distinctive gray/black camo, not the solid black uniforms of the colony's security people. Despite that, and the fact that they were wanted men, Tarragon didn't protest when Fuseli said, "Let's go."

-26-

As Fuseli and Tarragon made their way on foot toward the long, flat-roofed building that supported the wreck of the satellite dish, they came upon a young Colonial Forces soldier who sat in a corridor with his back propped against the wall and helmet off. He had tears in his eyes and his nose was bleeding heavily. He looked up at them forlornly, and Fuseli asked him if he'd been injured.

"I just want this thing out of my head," the young C-Forcer said, gesturing at his Merger device. "Something's wrong with it! I want it *out!*"

"Do you know what's happening at the Ceremony Chamber?" Fuseli asked.

"Everyone in there's changed," the young man said, bursting into sobs. "*Everyone!*"

"My God," Fuseli said to Tarragon. "So much for it only happening to people Merging alone." To the C-Forcer he said, "If you want that thing out, get your ass to the med unit and demand that robot remove it." He held out a hand to help hoist the soldier to his feet.

"Are you Captain Fuseli?"

"Yes. You have a problem with that?"

"No, sir … not at all!"

"Get going."

As Fuseli and Tarragon turned a corner into a new corridor, however, they heard the young man's voice shrieking with fear bordering on panic. They promptly reversed their course, running back the way they'd come and turning the corner to see two creatures galloping down the corridor at the man on six limbs. The C-Forcer was fumbling to get his sidearm out of its holster.

Fuseli noted that these two creatures were the same size, even their movements almost identical as if they were in sync. But he and Tarragon were in sync at that moment, too, and they both leveled their Drangs … which they'd set to shotgun mode, good for close-quarters combat.

"Get down!" Fuseli shouted, and the young man dropped to his belly.

The two Special Ops men opened up with shotgun blasts. The creature that, unbeknownst to them, had once been a teenager named Gabriela Bezerra was struck with a concentration of 00 buckshot square in the neck, tearing its head clean from its body. The bony sphere hit the floor and rolled, while the body—carried forward by momentum—collapsed upon the prone C-Forcer. The other one, formerly a boy named Gabriel, caught a blast from Tarragon in the exposed ribs of its chest, which flung it backwards. It went into a frenzy of kicking limbs for several moments, as if furious that it was in the process of dying … then died.

The C-Forcer finally got his Wolff .45 free from its holster, and took off at a mad dash.

Fuseli and Tarragon continued on toward the central building. They had never been to the Ceremony Chamber, but they knew it was underground and they knew there was one elevator, at least, in the satellite dish control center.

"I just hope that building is still accessible," Tarragon said as they hurried along. "Larck hit that dish *hard*."

In the dish control center, which Fuseli knew from the tour had previously been mostly automated, three human operators and one robot anxiously flitted from one control panel to another. Almost every monitor, whether physical or holographic, glowed red. Two Colonial Forcers guarded the elevator by which the tour had descended to the Plant that day, and though they grew alert when the Special Ops men burst into the room they didn't seem to want to engage … though Fuseli and Tarragon were ready for that, with any C-Forcers they encountered.

"What's the status of the dish up there?" Fuseli asked one of the frantic operators. "Is this building going to be compromised?"

"Well, there's no air up there for fires to keep burning, but we can't tell yet what kind of structural damage might have occurred. It seems like a ship collided with the dish!"

"I think you may be right." Fuseli moved toward the elevator. "You guarding against those things getting up here?"

"Yes, sir," one of the C-Forcers said.

"You have a problem with us going down to help contain the threat?"

The two posted guards exchanged a look.

"No, sir."

Fuseli and Tarragon rode in the roomy elevator cabin alone, and it deposited them in the Plant, where they were greeted by that large advertising screen that showed a continuous loop of workers assembling the starcraft that would be christened the E.C.S. Merger, at the Phosnoor Shipyard in Punktown. Seeing again that vessel composed of green alloy, Fuseli couldn't help but think of Izzy and her dream of the stars.

There was no night shift in the Plant, and the cleanroom enclosure at the center of the open-plan main room —where the Merger devices were assembled—stood empty of laborers.

Tarragon gestured with his Drang toward a door set into one wall of the main room, through which they had passed into the Merger Control Center that day. "We should go in there right now and shoot a couple of rockets into those brainframe servers."

"Larck made an executive decision to take out the dish," Fuseli said, "but I think us willfully destroying those servers might be a step beyond our authority. Besides, we don't know what effect it might have on these people's Mergers … which are already malfunctioning as it is, apparently." Fuseli heard a distant, continuous commotion somewhere up ahead, and motioned with his Drang in that direction. "Come on—that's the way."

They moved toward the entrance to a corridor, which the minister named Moussa had told them led to rooms wherein new Mergers were tested, including the smaller prototype unit. Fuseli and Tarragon bypassed several closed doors set in either wall, focused instead on a door at the corridor's end. They opened this, and found two more Colonial Forcers stationed in another corridor just outside. The soldiers, on edge, whirled at the Special Ops men but fortunately maintained their composure enough to withhold fire. In this corridor, the commotion they'd heard was so much louder, and of a hellish quality.

"Where's the Ceremony Chamber?" Fuseli asked.

"Can't you tell?" one of the C-Forcers said, pointing with his Drang down the blank, narrow corridor.

"Keep this door covered," Tarragon said. "Can't let these things spread through the colony."

"That's the idea, sir."

With that, Tarragon and Fuseli turned to run toward that chaos of noise.

A short while earlier, Marco Zarate had felt as though he were *ejected* from the Merge, so abruptly was he shocked out of it ... like a diver surfacing too quickly, painfully, from the ocean depths. Upon being thrust back into his body, he had gasped in air as if for the entirety of the Merge he'd been holding his breath, but as soon as he could fill his lungs he screamed. He wasn't even sure why.

He wasn't the only one. Beside him, Fhuum had jolted up into a sitting position on the spiral walkway, too, and her Choom mouth was like a cavern as she threw back her head and wailed. Zarate looked at her, as all the others screamed around them, their voices combining into one deafening howl of madness that was in itself a kind of Merge.

As he stared at Fhuum with his eyes bulging in his head, he saw the corners of her wide Choom mouth tear even wider. Wider. Until the top half of her face, long green-dyed hair rooted into its scalp, slid off the back of her skull like a cowl. The rest of her naked body was quaking violently ... shaking off the rest of her unneeded vestments of flesh.

In horror, his scream never-ending, Zarate lifted his arms before his face to see what was happening to them, and watched his hands detach from the stumps of his wrists and fall away like those dislodged from a mannequin. A moment later, the bones of both forearms split away from each other with a crack, their flesh ripping and spraying his own blood into his face. This was the last thing Zarate saw—with his human organs of vision, in any case—as the mask of his face was rent down the middle and his skull seemed to inflate, a complex pattern of linked hexagons rising up on it as if this design been hidden away inside him all his life.

His scream—all their combined screams—was finally cut off, but seconds later it was replaced by a language of high clicks and guttural popping noises. And all these voices were raised to the Ceremony Chamber's domed ceiling, too, in one unified expression of rage and despair.

But, it was not longer the despair of human beings. Those souls and the bodies that had housed them were gone. Replaced. And no one resented that turn of events more than the nearly one hundred beings—called the

Nought by ignorant humans—that found themselves transported into this circular chamber now.

-27-

The corridor they'd entered ended in double doors that opened into a large, brightly-lit locker room, and as the Special Ops men rushed toward this Fuseli took note of another elevator in this corridor by which the Hydrans could descend to the underground level. He and Tarragon plunged into the changing area and cut through it, following the sounds of battle.

Ahead, they saw six Colonial Forces soldiers clustered around another set of open double doors. Two stood in the doorway itself, their assault engines sputtering automatic fire into what Fuseli figured was the Ceremony Chamber, while the other four stood ready for action should anything get past those two. From beyond that open doorway came a cacophony of gunfire, human shouts and screams, and the clicking voices of dozens of creatures ... sounding like a chorus of insects from some nightmare's version of a jungle.

The C-Forcers only threw Fuseli and Tarragon quick looks as they approached, afraid to take their eyes off the room beyond.

"Let us get past," Fuseli told them.

"You sure about that?" one of the soldiers shouted over the chaos.

"You ever see action before this?" Tarragon asked.

"No, sir!"

"Then move!"

The two soldiers blocking the doorway cut their fire long enough for Fuseli and Tarragon to enter the Ceremony Chamber, Fuseli darting to the left and Tarragon to the right.

They found themselves standing on the encircling upper edge of a kind of amphitheater, with a ramp that spiraled down to its center. Spaced along this rim were about a dozen Colonial Forcers, all firing their Drangs into what appeared like a pit leading straight to hell, from which its demons sought escape. Within the pit swarmed a mass of alien bodies, crawling across not only their own shattered dead but also the corpses of several C-Forcers they had leaped up and dragged down from the rim. The spiral walkway was almost obscured from view under these seething bodies, along with all the scattered mounds of wet flesh the creatures had shed in the process of remaking their bodies. The very center of the spiral, a blank depression, had turned into a pool of blood. In the end, such was Colony Hydra's fount of knowledge.

One creature sprang onto the back of one of its brethren, and from there propelled itself through the air toward Tarragon. He stepped back, narrowly avoiding having his legs slashed by its hooked forelimbs, and rewarded the thing for its efforts by blasting it in the lower face with his Drang still in shotgun mode. Its four mandibles went flying off in different directions, and with its head barely attached the creature tumbled back down into the pit. Tarragon had no way of knowing that he had just killed what had once been a Choom woman named Fhuum.

Fuseli considered switching his Drang to mini rockets, to take out more of the creatures quickly, but he didn't want to risk compromising the atmosphere in this room by potentially breaching a wall. In any case, the fusillade of bullets was taking its toll, as more and more dead creatures joined the heaps of their fellows. On the other side of the domed chamber, however, Fuseli saw one of the entities leap up and embed its claws in one of the C-Forcers, wrenching him off the rim into the pit … where others tore into him savagely. He didn't scream for long.

One creature actually made it up onto the rim between Fuseli and Tarragon, but that was where the two C-Forcers blocked the doorway, and they both sprayed the thing liberally with their flashing Drangs. Fuseli looked over at the entity as it was literally shot to pieces, saw its disconnected head roll back down into the pit. It was impossible for him to spot in only a glimpse—and the creatures' implants were almost swallowed up by the bone of their oversized skulls, in any case—but this individual had worn a Merger that was much smaller than all the rest. Just the size of a coin.

At last, there was no movement at all amongst the indecipherable tangle of bodies, the clicking voices had ceased, and a haze of smoke hung over the scene. Immediately, two soldiers removed their helmets as if suddenly claustrophobic, gasping for air. A third removed his helmet, dropped to all fours on the rim and vomited.

Fuseli saw there were a few deep slashes among the soldiers, the worst appearing to be a long gash in the front of one C-Forcer's thigh. He made his way along the rim to this person, setting down his Drang to assist them, even as they removed their helmet to reveal the face of Corporal Eva Gerling. She was wincing, having bravely held her position throughout the incident until now, when she could give in to her pain.

Quickly removing and tossing aside his own helmet, Fuseli caught Gerling's arm as she began to sag. Her eyes widened in surprise at recognizing him. "Corporal Gerling," he said to her, "you have utterly failed at getting all four of your limbs torn up. You still have one intact." He put his arm around her waist to hold her up.

"Captain!" Gerling said. Her voice sounded as though she were edging toward blacking out. "They told us to watch out for you … you were trying to escape on a shuttle … "

"Well here I am, so you don't need to look. Hey, let's do this piggyback. We'll get someone to call a med tram over here."

Gerling did as he suggested, wrapping her arms around Fuseli's neck from behind. He stood up with her and worked his way along the rim back toward the double doors. The other soldiers arranged there respectfully made room for him.

Tarragon stepped forward, arms held out. "Let me, Captain."

"Okay, Morris. You're stronger anyway."

Tarragon took Gerling into his arms like a child, and the guards at the door stepped aside to let them through. As he followed, Fuseli said to the soldiers, "Call the med unit. Tell them to get a tram down here, and to expect injuries. I'll be lending them a hand."

One of the C-Forcers put his hand on Fuseli's arm to stop him, and Fuseli tensed up, expecting this battle not to be over with, after all, but the soldier said to him gravely, "Captain … we just got word that Minister Abbas is dead."

"*What?* How?"

"One of those things got into his office through a power conduit."

"I thought you were going to tell me he shot himself," Fuseli said, slipping past to continue on his way. "That would have been the decent thing to do."

As Tarragon went on ahead, carrying Gerling, Fuseli paused to look back into the haze that obscured the horrors in that amphitheater turned pit of hell. "All those poor people. They just wanted some kind of peace … and Gaithersburg sold it to them as a drug."

Finally he remembered that all this time General Stroud had continued to watch events unfold from his wrist comp. It must have been too chaotic, really, to make sense of. He raised his device and unmuted it.

"Jesus, Bob," was all Stroud could say.

"Their Ceremony Chamber is contained," Fuseli reported, "but there are others loose through the colony that are going to have to be tracked down. They lost some C-Forcers in here, but there are still enough of them left to handle that. I'm going on to the med unit to treat the wounded."

"Two platoons are on their way as we speak. Are those people still posing a threat to you, Bob?"

"Doesn't seem like it. I don't know if it's because they've got bigger worries on their hands, or if it's because the Mergers have lost their grip on their minds. Also … Abbas is dead."

"Say what?" Stroud exclaimed. "Hey … you didn't—"

"No," Fuseli said, on the move again to catch up with Tarragon. He couldn't help but chuckle wearily. "It wasn't me."

-28-

Since the soldiers who had dwelt at Colony Hydra—though considered citizens—had still officially been members of the Colonial Forces and not employees of Gaithersburg, Incorporated, it was General Stroud who stepped forward to assign a new security chief to replace Murgan Larck … and that was Lieutenant Morris Tarragon. At least for now, until the mess at Colony Hydra could be sorted out. The Earth Colonies network had a lot to discuss, yet, with the board of directors of Gaithersburg.

Tarragon busied himself with leading patrols of the newly arrived one hundred C-Forcers, scouring the colony for the remaining creatures. In so doing they swiftly eliminated—among others that had transformed—the salon worker named Trinh, and the maintenance tech named Amjad Idrissi.

The new Head Minister, Sonya Kennedy—quickly voted in by her fellow ministers—had assured those investigating the happenings at Colony Hydra that none of the cabinet had been aware of Rusul Abbas's plan to threaten Captain Fuseli and Lieutenant Tarragon with death, and so far no charges had been brought against any of them. For his part, Fuseli had his doubts, and wondered if any of the ministers would ever be required to take a truth scan to back up their claims.

He wondered, too, how badly Gaithersburg, Incorporated would suffer from all this. It was perhaps too powerful a company, with its hands in too many areas, to collapse completely … but he had serious doubts about the E.C.S. Merger ever seeing the stars.

In addition, the Earth Colonies government itself had accepted Fuseli's recommendation, presented through Stroud, that every citizen of Colony Hydra should have their Merger device removed. It was ordained that the deep space satellite dish was not to be replaced, and the brainframe servers in the Merger Control Room were to be dismantled. In the end, Colony Hydra was still an Earth Colonies base, and subject to its dictates.

Fuseli himself helped the robot the colonists called Florence remove the Mergers from all the colonists—beginning with the children, at his insistence—and he found it significant that not one colonist he spoke with offered any resistance or expressed any resentment about having their implant extracted. He again had to wonder if the master system they had all been linked to had exerted some controlling influence over their minds, programmed there by the mysterious Klaus Gaithersburg himself. Or … was it simply that they'd seen too much death, and lost too many loved ones, to want those devices screwed into their own heads any longer?

At the moment, Fuseli and Florence stood on opposite sides of a table upon which Eva Gerling lay stretched out on her belly, her face inserted into an opening like that of a massage table as Florence lowered an overhead arm to her Merger so as to withdraw its pins.

"You'll be back to work in no time, Eva," Fuseli told her. "There's still hope for you getting that fourth limb of yours torn up."

"I'll do my best, sir."

"I dare say, Dr. Fuseli," Florence said to him, "you and I make a great team. Perhaps when this colony resumes normal activities, you'll consider staying on for a while to help us improve our medical facility."

"I would like to get a qualified human being in here to run the show," Fuseli said, looking up at the machine. "After all, you had quite a hand in all the harm that was done here, Florence … implanting these people with these insidious contraptions."

"As you, ah, know, Doctor … I only, uh, do exactly as I am told." The Asian woman's face on the robot's head screen winked at him.

"You know, Florence," Fuseli said, "I think once I find a good med chief to bring in here, my recommendation will be to have you reprogrammed to clean toilets."

As he turned away from the table, the mouth of Florence's avatar hung open in a look of dismay.

On his wrist comp Fuseli checked on Tarragon's whereabouts, and arranged for them to meet for a break at that little cafeteria near the guest dorm rooms they still made use of.

The two men carried cups of coffee to one of the cafeteria's little tables and sat. Tarragon looked smart in a fresh uniform and his black Special Ops beret. Fuseli had taken to wearing his own beret, as well.

"I'll probably be staying on here longer than you, Captain," Tarragon said.

"Could be. I expect I'll have to present my report directly to the E.C. on Earth. Not that I'll mind being returned to Earth, for once."

"For my part, I'm eager to get back to Punktown."

Fuseli chuckled. "Listen to us … pining for those two hellholes."

"Pining for the people waiting for us," Tarragon corrected.

Sipping his coffee, Fuseli watched a couple enter the cafeteria to buy some treats from the vending machines for their two young children. All four of them were devoid of Mergers, and he remembered removing the devices from those two children himself. The father, with his curly black hair, put him in mind somewhat of Marco Zarate. Thinking of Zarate made him think, in turn, of other losses.

"Past couple years I've been socking away money to take a nice vacation when I was clear for one," Fuseli said. "I'm thinking now, though, I'm going to send my vacation stash to a certain Gurm chieftain who could use that money to help his village, once I find his contact information." Having said this, Fuseli held Tarragon's gaze for a meaningful few moments.

Finally, Tarragon blew out a long breath. "Ah, to hell with it … guess I'll contribute the money I've been socking away for a vacation, too."

"Your new Choom girlfriend will get a big frown on her face if you do."

"She'll just have to understand," said Tarragon. "What about your girlfriend?"

"Rhan and I won't be free to take any vacations together for a while yet, anyway. Wherever they send her next, though, I plan to be right beside her."

"Until the next shitshow they call you away to, right?"

"There's always that, Morris," Fuseli agreed. "There's always that."

About the Author

Jeffrey Thomas is the author of the dark science fiction series Punktown, which was introduced with the collection *Punktown* (Ministry of Whimsy Press, 2000) and includes the novels *Monstrocity* (Prime Books, 2003; Bram Stoker Award finalist), *Deadstock* (Solaris Books, 2007; John W. Campbell Award finalist), and *Blue War* (Solaris Books, 2008). His other books include the short story collection *The Unnamed Country* (Word Horde, 2019), the novel *The American* (JournalStone, 2020), and the Hades Trilogy (Weird House Press, 2023). His stories have been reprinted in *The Year's Best Horror Stories XXII* (editor, Karl Edward Wagner), *The Year's Best Fantasy and Horror #14* (editors, Ellen Datlow and Terri Windling), and *Year's Best Weird Fiction #1* (editors, Laird Barron and Michael Kelly). Thomas lives in Massachusetts.

About the Artist

Frank Walls is an American artist best known for his dark surrealism, fantasy illustration, and heavy metal musicianship. He spent the 90s screaming into a microphone for bands like Embalmer and Hateworks, and producing art for others like Incantation and Crypt Kicker. In 2004 he graduated from the Cleveland Institute of Art with a BFA in illustration and went on to work in the gaming industry for companies like Fantasy Flight Games and Wizards of the Coast, as well as creating cover art for authors such as Jeffrey Thomas, Jeff Strand, and Shane McKenzie. He now hails from Hawaii where he pursues his passion for painting, teaches art and design, and works as a freelance illustrator.

www.ingramcontent.com/pod-product-compliance
Lightning Source LLC
Chambersburg PA
CBHW030326020726
47493CB00004B/1172
9781888993813